"You know what I think?"

Alexis angled her head to look up at him. The deep, dark centers of his eyes picked up the light and reflected it back at her. "No…" she said on a breath. "What *do* you think?"

Graham stopped walking. He clasped her arm and turned her to face him. She glanced up at him, expectant and knowing.

"I think…" He stroked the curve of her jaw with the tip of his finger. A shiver rippled through her. "I think that we make a formidable couple."

Couple? But before she could process the implication, he'd lifted her chin, and the world around her was blocked out as he lowered his head and touched his lips to hers.

Testing…teasing…tasting…taking.

He cupped the back of her head and eased her into the kiss, deeper and sweeter.

Heat coursed through her even as she shivered against him. He pulled her closer.

Books by Donna Hill

Harlequin Kimani Romance

Love Becomes Her
If I Were Your Woman
After Dark
Sex and Lies
Seduction and Lies
Temptation and Lies
Longing and Lies
Private Lessons
Spend My Life with You
Secret Attraction
Sultry Nights
Everything Is You
Mistletoe Baby

DONNA HILL

began writing novels in 1990. Since that time she has had more than forty titles published, which include full length novels and novellas. Two of her novels and one novella were adapted for television. She has won numerous awards for her body of work. She is also the editor of five novels, two of which were nominated for awards. She easily moves from romance to erotica, horror, comedy and women's fiction. She was the first recipient of the RT Book Reviews Trailblazer Award, won an *RT Book Reviews* Career Achievement Award and currently teaches writing at the Frederick Douglass Creative Arts Center.

Donna lives in Brooklyn with her family. Visit her website at www.donnahill.com.

MISTLETOE, *Baby*

DONNA HILL

⟨H⟩ **HARLEQUIN**® KIMANI™ ROMANCE

Recycling programs
for this product may
not exist in your area.

ISBN-13: 978-0-373-86332-7

MISTLETOE, BABY

HARLEQUIN®
™ www.Harlequin.com

Printed in U.S.A.

Dear Reader,

With the holiday season on the horizon, can love be far behind? Many of you may remember the feisty Alexis Montgomery, the best friend of Naomi Campbell from *Private Lessons*. Well, Alexis is back with a full-blown story of her own, and all of her rules about crossing the lines of professionalism slowly dissolve when she meets Graham Stone.

I loved bringing Alexis to full life with her own story. Even more exciting was creating the sexy British hero Graham Stone, whose passion for righting the wrongs of the underclass is eclipsed only by his passion for Alexis.

Although this is a holiday-themed book, it has a story line that will resonate with many and showcase the critical issues of undereducating our youth, as well as spark conversation about what we can do as a community to make it better. Alexis and Graham are leading that charge—at least when they can keep their hands off of each other!

I hope you enjoy every page. I love hearing from you. Drop me a line on my Facebook page, www.facebook.com/donnahillwriter, and be sure to join my fan page, at www.facebook.com/donnahillfans, for prizes and the inside scoop on upcoming books and projects.

Until next time,

Donna

Chapter 1

Her farewell party was in full swing. The kisses and hugs had been given, the toasts made and the tears shed. Now it was on to the business of drinking and eating—in that order. Her staff managed to commandeer the very dignified Presidential conference suite and transformed it into an "after five" lounge that was complete with bartenders, waiters and a DJ.

Even as she looked around at the people that she'd considered family for the past five years, and knew that she would miss them dearly, there was an undeniable bubble of excitement that wanted the day to be over, her bags packed and the jet taking off from Hartsfield-Jackson International Airport en route to New York City. Atlanta was a great place. It was her home. She'd built a stellar career in academia rising up in the ranks at Atlanta College to her current position as Dean of Academic Affairs, but as the old saying goes, "Always leave them wanting more."

She was at the top of her game. The name Alexis Montgomery was always spoken of in the highest regard. Word had gotten around that she excelled at what she did and she was made an offer that she couldn't refuse.

During the past six months she'd been flown out to New York to meet with the board of directors at R.E.A.L., toured their Midtown Manhattan office and talked terms. After weeks of negotiation she'd signed off on her five-year contract.

Alexis brought the glass of champagne to her lips and smiled at the throng of faces. She'd left the college in better shape than when she'd stepped in. She had much to be proud of and she had every intention of making her mark in New York the same way she'd done it in Atlanta. A thrill of anticipation coursed through her. In a little more than a week her new life would begin. *Look out, New York—this Southern Belle is on her way.*

"You realize there's really no one to fill those high heels of yours," came a rugged whisper in her ear.

Alexis casually angled her head to the right. A secret smile moved across her mouth and a light of something more than "we're only colleagues" lit the dark embers of her brown eyes. "I'm sure you only mean that in the most professional sense." The corner of her mouth flickered in a barely there grin.

"If you say so." He lifted his chin in the direction of her almost-empty glass. "Refill?"

She shrugged her bare shoulder. "Sure. It's my party, right?"

"Be right back."

Alexis watched him walk away and smiled to herself

as several of her female colleagues scoped him out, as well. Ian Matthews was without a doubt a *very* eligible bachelor. He was the whole package; six feet plus, well built, with a walk like Denzel, a mind like Einstein, sweet milk chocolate *all over,* funny, well-endowed and an expert at using his "equipment"; a tenured professor, chair of his department and actually an all-around decent guy to boot. They'd been discreetly seeing each other off and on for nearly a year. But something kept Alexis from committing, although Ian said that he wanted to. She honestly cared about him. She was close to being addicted to the crazy sex that they had, but something was missing.

That missing something was the thing that had allowed her to sign on the dotted line. With her mother's passing, her best friend Naomi Clarke all happily married and relocated to Virginia, and that spark she was looking for in a relationship still out of reach, there was nothing more to keep her in Atlanta.

Ian returned with her drink.

"Thank you."

Ian's voice rose above the hum of conversation. "Can I have everyone's attention for a moment?"

By degrees the room quieted and the guests all turned in his direction.

"What are you doing?" Alexis whispered through clenched teeth that doubled as a smile.

He gave her a long, stirring look and her heart nearly jumped out of her chest. Her face heated.

"I want to make a toast to the most brilliant, beautiful, decent woman that I know. Her departure is going to leave a big gap here at Atlanta College and a bigger one in my heart." He pressed his hand dramatically on his chest.

There was a collective gasp of wide-eyed surprise for some and a "knew it all along" expression on the faces of a few.

Ian turned to her with a smile that could steal her heart if she let it. For a moment she doubted her decision. He raised his glass and the rest of the guests did the same. "To Alexis. Wishing you much success and happiness, and here's hoping that you take a big bite out of the Big Apple. Cheers!"

"Cheers!"

Alexis mouthed her thank-yous and sipped from her glass.

"I meant what I said."

Alexis gazed up at him. "Ian…"

They were mere inches apart. Their voices were low and intimate.

"No need to take it any further. I wanted you to know that what I feel for you isn't only in the bedroom." He grinned. "I'm not going to lie and tell you I'll wait but I will say that I'm not in a hurry to look."

She pushed out a breath. "You are determined not to make this easy for me."

"When has anything between us been easy?"

She lifted her glass. "Touché."

"I'm so sorry I couldn't be there for your send-off."

Alexis adjusted the phone between her ear and shoulder while she put the last few items in her suitcase. "Naomi, the last place I expected you to be was at my going-away party."

"I know but still. You came to see me last week."

"That's different. You just had a baby last week. And I had to see my brand-new goddaughter before I left and make sure my bestie was all right."

"I'm exhausted and achy but every time I look at April my heart swells. I still can't believe that she's here and she's mine and Brice's."

Alexis listened to the awe and joy in her friend's voice. She was happy for Naomi and Brice. The two friends still laughed about how Naomi and Brice had met in Antigua—the trip that Alexis was supposed to go on with her and didn't—with Naomi pretending to be someone else the entire time, only for Brice to wind up in Naomi's classroom when she returned to her real life as a professor at Atlanta College. Ever since Naomi had married Brice and moved away, and continued to regale her with the wonders of marriage and now motherhood, she found herself wondering if she would ever find that kind of happiness, that all-consuming love that lit up a room. Every now and again she thought it might be Ian, but that spark never quite reached that level of intensity.

On the other hand, there was never a shortage of men in Alexis's life. If anything there was always a surplus with one in the wings. Things slowed down when Ian moved into the picture. But...

"You call me when you get to New York," Naomi was saying.

Alexis blinked back to the moment. "Of course. As soon as I touch down. Not sure when I'm going to get back to see you and my goddaughter."

"Don't worry about us. You just go to New York and kick ass."

Alexis chuckled. "I plan to. Listen, give my baby a kiss and one for Brice, too."

"Gonna miss you, girl."

"Same here. But that's why we have planes and Skype and FaceTime."

They laughed.

"True."

Alexis could hear the baby crying in the background. "Go take care of April. I'll call you."

"Safe travels, sis."

"Thanks."

"Love you."

"Love you, too."

Alexis hung up the phone with a soft sigh. She looked around her bedroom. She'd had some pretty happy times in here, she mused wryly. She zipped up her last suitcase just as a car horn honked out front.

She walked to the window facing the street and pulled the curtain aside. Her cab was out front. Thankfully, she'd shipped the majority of her belongings a week ago, leaving her with only one suitcase, her carry-on and her purse. She checked to make sure she had her ID, credit cards, cell phone and laptop. She took one last look around, turned off the lights, grabbed her bags and left her old life behind.

Chapter 2

Alexis had to give props to R.E.A.L. The organization—Realize Excellence Achievement Leadership—had arranged to have her furniture and clothing moved, they'd found her an apartment in New York and they'd gotten her a first-class ticket. She could easily get used to this kind of treatment.

The moment she stepped off the airplane and into the JFK terminal she could feel the energy that always seemed to hum beneath the surface in New York. It was hard to explain to anyone who had not experienced it, but it was similar to turning up the volume on your life or walking into a dark room and someone flipping on the bright lights.

She rode along with the other arriving passengers on the down escalator to baggage claim. As soon as she stepped off of the escalator she was stunned to see a navy blue suited young man holding up a sign with her name on it. She grinned. R.E.A.L. was pulling out all of the stops. She was totally impressed.

She walked up to the driver.

"Hi, I'm Alexis Montgomery."

"Ms. Montgomery." He gave a short nod. "Michael. I'm your driver. I'll help you with your bags and then I'll go and get the car."

"Great. Hopefully it won't take too long." She headed in the direction of carousel three with Michael at her side.

"How was your flight?"

"Very nice, thanks to a first-class ticket. The organization treats its employees very well."

They stopped in front of the carousel that had already begun to fill with luggage.

"Yes, it does."

Shortly her bags came around on the belt. Michael took them and walked to the exit. "If you wouldn't mind waiting a moment, I'll bring the car."

"I can walk with you to the car."

"No worries. I'll be right back."

She inwardly shrugged. *Fine with me.* She walked over to a nearby bench, sat down and watched arriving travelers run into the arms of waiting loved ones. She experienced a momentary twinge of melancholy, knowing there were no open arms to greet her, just a furnished apartment in an unfamiliar city. She sniffed, opened her purse in search of her cigarettes and then remembered that she'd recently quit and suddenly wished that she hadn't and took out a stick of gum instead. She glanced around, took in the sights and sounds. Although it was early May, it was a balmy seventy-five degrees. *Almost like home,* she thought.

Just then a black Lincoln pulled up in front of her and Michael quickly got out. He reached for her carry-on and opened the passenger door. Alexis slid into the roomy interior and gasped in alarm.

"Sorry, I didn't mean to startle you. Please. Sit."

Alexis's pulse raced. She settled herself opposite her surprise guest.

"Graham Stone." He extended his hand.

Her eyes widened. "Graham Stone, CEO of R.E.A.L.?" Her hand, of its own volition, found its way into his. His long fingers wrapped around her hand and it was as if he'd cut off the oxygen to her brain.

He grinned and even in the dim interior she could see his eyes sparkle. Her stomach fluttered. She pressed her knees together to silence the lady that had jumped up and started to purr.

"Guilty as charged. My flight from London came in just before yours. I told Michael to find you. Much more efficient for him to take the both of us than to have you take a cab in a strange city."

"I…appreciate that."

Graham leaned back against the plush leather of the car. His steel-gray suit was in that new slender cut and it clearly outlined the long lean lines of his body. He looked her over in slow motion. "I have to apologize for this impromptu meeting," he said, and she caught the barely there British accent. "It was unfortunate that I was out of town when you came in to meet with the board last month. And that we couldn't 'meet' on the conference call."

"I was beginning to think that maybe you were only a voice or a figment of everyone's imagination."

Graham chuckled, the kind of deep robust sound that made you all warm inside.

"Not the first time I've heard that. Unfortunately, my focus is on building the organization and getting the kids of the inner city into the kind of schools that they deserve. I don't always have time for the elbow rubbing and schmoozing. I prefer to remain behind the scenes as much as possible, in addition to which the work involves a great deal of travel." As he spoke he stared directly at her, never averting his gaze. It was mesmerizing as much as it was unsettling.

Alexis cleared her throat. "And that's why you hired me?"

"Yes. I want you to be the face of R.E.A.L. and I need your expertise."

Want and *need* had never sounded so erotic. She shifted in her seat and linked her long fingers together and rested them on her lap. The pure surprise of stepping into a car and meeting her very gorgeous boss for the first time completely threw her for a loop. She was accustomed to being in control of a situation and certainly in control of her thoughts—but not now. And what was that intoxicating scent he was wearing?

"At least you have the weekend to get comfortable—a little." He grinned.

"I'm looking forward to getting started," she managed.

He slowly nodded his head without taking his eyes off of her. "Good. I have several new projects waiting for you on your desk. You'll have to hit the ground running."

"I'm ready." The instant the words were out of her

mouth she wanted to pull them back. She knew what she'd said was simple and direct, but in her head they held a completely different meaning.

He stroked his clean-shaven chin with his thumb and forefinger and Alexis had the overwhelming need to open the window. It was as if someone had struck a match in her belly.

"Would you like something to drink?" he asked, jumping into her head.

She blinked and smiled. "That would be great. Thank you."

He reached into the minibar. "Water, juice, soda or something stronger?" He gazed across at her from beneath his lashes.

"Uh, water is fine."

He produced a bottle of water and plucked a glass from the holder, and handed both to her.

"Thank you." Somehow she managed to get the bottle open and pour it into her glass without making a mess and a fool out of herself. She was quite amazed actually as her fingers wavered between being board stiff or weak as wet noodles. When she lifted her head from the minor task she was rattled to see Graham looking at her with a bemused expression on his face.

"Are you always so intense?"

She straightened. "Intense?"

"Yes. You were working on that bottle as if it was the most important job you'd ever undertaken."

Her cheeks flushed. She lifted her chin. "You haven't seen me intense," she said, the hint of a taunt on her tongue.

Graham made a humming murmur in his throat. He angled his head to the side. His eyes creased ever so slightly at the corners. "Have they found a replacement for you at the college?"

"Not yet. The position has been posted. I'm sure they'll find someone reasonably soon."

"I'm sure they feel your loss already. You made a lot of important changes over there. Several of the departments missed the ax because of you."

At that moment she wasn't sure if she was seriously impressed or annoyed. The fact that she'd been able to work with the board and the department chairs to restructure without losing students or teachers was not common knowledge beyond the boardroom of Atlanta College. "How did you know all of that?"

"I make it my business to know everything there is to know about the people that get hired at your level. I also want to make certain that there is real substance behind the fancy words on a résumé and cover letter."

"I see." She now knew she was annoyed. What else did he know about her that wasn't on her résumé and didn't come out in the phone interview? Clearly it didn't matter if he was around to ask direct questions or not. He still got answers.

And then as if reading her mind he asked, "How did Ian take your leaving?"

Her eyes widened. "I beg your pardon?"

"Ian...Matthews. Isn't it?"

Her heart began to race. "Yes." Her response was as much a question as an answer.

"He was one of your references," he said as if in answer to the question that hovered on the tip of her tongue. "He had wonderful things to say about you and gave the impression that...you would be missed."

Her cheeks were on fire. A tight line formed between

her brows. "I don't recall giving Ian Matthews as a reference."

"You didn't. Whenever I'm interested in a potential candidate for the organization at the management level, I look into their surrounding circle of colleagues."

"So basically, screw what's on the reference letters."

The corner of his mouth lifted into a slight grin. "Well, let's be honest, what person who really wants a job would get reference letters or use references from someone who wouldn't say that they were wonderful?"

Her right brow arched. She almost laughed but didn't. He was actually right, but she'd never tell him that. "So who made these calls? *You?*"

"Yes. I generally do, but I felt it was even more important since I didn't have the pleasure of meeting you in person during your visit. You'll come to see in the days and months and hopefully years ahead that I'm a very hands-on person."

Her gaze dropped to his hands that rested casually on his thighs. She swallowed and nearly choked over the dry knot in her throat. She coughed and took a sip of water.

Graham moved forward, halfway reaching for her. "Are you all right?"

She nodded her head. "Yes," she managed. "Throat got really dry." She took another sip of water. She made herself look at him and forced a confident smile. "Fine. Really."

He leaned back in his seat, eyed her for a moment and then took out a pair of glasses from the inside breast pocket of his jacket, slipped them on and picked up a folder that was next to him on the seat. He flipped it open and began to read.

Glasses. Nice touch, she thought absently. He had

that whole *GQ* look down to an art form. He scanned through the papers in the folder and then handed them across to her, taking her a bit by surprise.

"Some easy weekend reading so that you won't come in cold on Monday." He lifted his chin in the direction of the folder. "Those are the plans for the upcoming projects. Some of the details were hammered out while I was in London. No one has seen them as yet. I'd like to get your take on it."

Alexis cleared her throat. "I'll let you know."

He gave a short nod just as the Lincoln cruised to a halt. "We're here."

Michael rounded the car and opened the door. He extended a hand to help her to her feet. Alexis stepped out onto Sutton Place. She glanced upward at the four- and five-story town houses that ran between Fifty-Seventh and Fifty-Eighth Streets, oozed style and sophistication and paid homage to the bygone era of the roaring '20s. The building boasted a long list of who's who from the financial world like the Vanderbilts and the Morgans of J. P. Morgan fame, and celebrities such as Marilyn Monroe, actress Sigourney Weaver, designer Kenneth Cole and architect I. M. Pei.

"I know originally that we were to set you up in Midtown," Graham was saying as he stepped out of the car to stand beside her. "A good friend of mine owns one of the apartments at 10 Sutton and he's never here. R.E.A.L. leased it from him. I hope you'll like it."

Okay, now she was speechless. She'd heard about Sutton Place, read about it and saw pictures of the stately homes and co-ops. Never in her wildest dreams did she imagine living there. She wanted to do the happy dance but was sure it would be inappropriate.

"Very nice. I'm sure it'll be fine," she said, with a slight wave of her hand as if she lived in million-dollar homes on a regular basis.

Michael retrieved her bags from the car and was met at the curb by the red-vested doorman complete with a luggage cart.

"Welcome back, Mr. Stone. How was your trip?"

"Very productive, Glen. Thanks. How've you been? Did your wife have the baby yet?"

"Any minute now," the young man said with a beaming smile. "And I really want to thank you for writing the scholarship letter for my niece."

Graham clapped Glen on the shoulder. "Not a problem. You just tell Misty to make us all proud."

"Oh, she will. I know she will."

Alexis took this all in as Michael and Glen loaded the suitcases onto the cart. Graham Stone *lived here* or did he just know the doorman? She could hear her voice rising in her head. Michael took Graham's bags and added them with the others, answering her unspoken question.

"I want you to look out for Ms. Montgomery. She'll be taking over Vernon's apartment on three. Alexis Montgomery, Glen Johnson."

"Nice to meet you." Alexis shook his hand.

"Ms. Montgomery." He gave her a short nod and a smile. "Well, that explains the cleaning company and all the moving. I thought Mr. Vernon was finally coming back," Glen said as he began pushing the cart to the entrance.

"Hopefully they did a good job," Graham said as he strode forward. He stopped at the front desk and shook hands with the man behind the counter, took a set of keys and waved Alexis over.

"Alexis Montgomery, this is Milton, the building's concierge. Whatever you need, he'll help you." He placed the keys in Alexis's hand.

"Welcome to 10, Ms. Montgomery." He produced a brochure from beneath the desk and handed it to her. "It contains a list of amenities as well as information on local services."

"Thank you."

Graham had walked off and was in conversation with a woman who'd just gotten off the elevator. He kissed her cheek and held the elevator door for Michael and Glen who stepped aside to let Alexis board.

The door swooshed closed behind them. Alexis was working hard at being cool but it was becoming more difficult by the minute.

Michael pressed the button. Within moments the doors opened onto her floor. The corridor was as exquisite and lush as a staged photograph. The cool spearmint-colored carpet made the hallway virtually soundproof and exuded a sensation of tranquillity. Michael and Glen led the way toward the front door. Alexis's heartbeat escalated with each step. Graham lingered a few steps behind. He was busy texting on his phone.

Alexis stood in front of apartment 3. She fiddled with the keys until she located the correct one and then inserted it into the lock and turned.

The front door opened onto a spacious living space flanked by floor-to-ceiling windows that rose to meet cathedral ceilings. She slowly walked in, feeling as if she were entering someone else's life. It was ultramodern with splashes of noir chic. The wood floors sparkled. The open floor plan showcased a chef's kitchen complete with an oversized stainless-steel refrigerator, dishwasher, double oven and a center island with a sink in the center and seating for four. The overhead cabinets wrapped around the kitchen and were inset with opaque glass. At the far end of the living room was a metal spiral staircase that led downstairs.

"Where would you like your bags, Ms. Montgomery?" Glen asked.

Alexis blinked rapidly, gave her head a slight shake and turned to face the three men who stood behind her.

"Umm." She looked around quickly.

"The bedrooms are downstairs," Graham offered, briefly glancing up from his cell phone.

She looked at him with a raised brow of question.

"My apartment is similar," he said by way of an answer. "I'm on top of you."

Her insides quivered. *On top of me.* Her thoughts galloped off at breakneck speed and nearly dragged her along with them. She drew in a breath. "Downstairs, then," she said. "Thanks."

Glen and Michael unloaded the cart and began taking the bags to the lower level.

"This apartment is fabulous."

"They've upgraded all of the units in the past five years." He looked casually around. "Vernon did a nice job with the space."

"How long have you lived here?"

"Almost eight years."

Glen and Michael returned. "Your bags are in the master bedroom," Glen offered.

"Thank you so much."

He nodded his head and hurried out, shutting the door softly behind him.

"We'll let you get settled," Graham said and was

walking to the door before all of the words were out of his mouth. Michael reached the door before him and opened it.

"Thank you again," Alexis called out.

Graham raised a hand in acknowledgment just before the door closed behind them.

Alexis released a breath of pure, giddy delight. She grabbed the handrail and hurried downstairs. She reached the bottom and stopped in her tracks. The bottom of the stairs opened onto a sitting room. The walls had built-in shelves with cabinets underneath. Beyond the sitting room was a full bathroom on the other side of the stairs. Down the narrow hallway was another kitchen—smaller than the one upstairs but just as finely detailed and equipped. Opposite the kitchen was a formal dining room. The next room over was a good-size bedroom and around a short corner was the master bedroom with a cedar walk-in closet complete with en suite.

Now this is off the charts. She opened and closed doors and explored all the nooks and crannies. Wait until she told Naomi. She had definitely hit pay dirt. Dream job, dream apartment in the city that never sleeps and a boss that… Her breath caught in her chest. She wouldn't think about that. Couldn't think about it. Instinctively her eyes rose and she imagined Graham walking through his apartment—*on top of her.*

Chapter 3

Graham loosened his tie and shrugged out of his jacket while he walked from the entrance straight to his bedroom. He'd opted to keep his bedroom on the lower level as well, with the main level reserved for dining and entertaining. He'd purchased the apartment almost eight years earlier but he was still unaccustomed to the luxury of it all. His former life was a far cry from the one he lived now and even though the battle scars weren't visible they remained.

He hung his jacket on the hook behind his bedroom door, opened his walk-in closet and slid his suitcase inside, only taking out his shaving kit. He'd deal with unpacking later. He tugged his tie all the way off and hung it on the tie rack, stepped out of his shoes and placed them on the shelf with the others then shut the closet door. Two rows of shoes. Sometimes he had to look more than once to believe it.

What he wanted was a cold beer, to stretch out on the couch and catch a Knicks game. He stripped out of his shirt, tossed it in the laundry bag and hung his slacks up with his jacket on the back of the door. He'd have Milton send everything over to the dry cleaner in the morning along with his other suit and the shirts from his trip.

He grabbed a white T-shirt from the middle drawer of his dresser and a pair of navy blue sweatpants that were faded and as soft as a baby's blanket from years of washing and wearing. The U.S. Navy insignia on the right pocket was barely visible. He headed back upstairs with the hope that there was at least one beer in the fridge. He lucked out.

He plucked the bottle of Coors from the shelf and took a quick look at the contents inside the fridge and then the deep freezer, packed tight with meats, fish and chicken. A ball of tension knotted in his stomach. He walked over to the pantry and pulled the door open and then the cabinets one by one. His heart thundered in his chest. *Not enough. There wasn't enough.* For a moment his right hand trembled ever so slightly as he ran it across the rows of canned goods, boxed items, bags of pastas, jars of sauces and columns of spices. What he saw was half full, not abundance. Rationally he understood that, but emotionally he saw empty. He felt pangs of hunger and an unreasonable fear that made his heart race.

He forced himself to close the cabinet door. He twisted off the cap on the beer bottle and took a long, calming swallow. He squeezed his eyes shut and willed his pulse to slow. By degrees he began to relax and the images of his past slowly receded.

Graham crossed the room, picked up the remote from the coffee table and aimed it at the wall-mounted flat-screen television. He surfed until he found the game before setting down the remote. Second quarter. The Knicks were down by ten. He shook his head, chuckled and stretched out on the couch.

When a commercial played across the screen showcasing a quartet of beautiful women celebrating with a night out on the town, he thought of Alexis Montgomery and wondered how she would fit in with his team and the pace of the New York lifestyle.

He'd read her résumé. It was impressive to say the least. She had an MBA in finance and a doctorate in education. She spoke fluent Spanish, French and was competent in Mandarin. She was well traveled, well-read and well respected, and she was definitely easy on the eyes. He was eager to hear her thoughts on the proposal that he'd given her to review. He liked the sound of her voice, the even throatiness of it and the way she looked directly at him. And even the way she tackled opening that bottle of water. He smiled and took another long swallow of beer just as the game resumed.

In a little under two hours, Alexis had unpacked and began to familiarize herself with her new digs. She'd set up her laptop in the smaller of the two bedrooms that she would use as her office. She'd verified that the cable was on and the internet was working—all courtesy of R.E.A.L. There were the basic staples in the fridge and pantry but she needed to go food shopping, especially to pick up some of the things that she liked. She had no idea where to go but maybe Milton could tell her where the nearest supermarket was.

She shoved her feet into her sneakers, grabbed her purse and dropped her cell phone inside. She palmed the weight of her new keys and grinned as she wrapped her fingers around them and her new life. She took another look around before heading out of the door.

Milton was reading the *New York Times* when she approached the front desk. "Ms. Montgomery." He rested the paper on the desk. "How can I help you?"

"I was wondering if you could tell me where I could find the nearest supermarket."

His right brow rose momentarily. "Certainly." He frowned. "Should I get you a car service?"

"How far is it?"

"Several blocks."

She smiled. "I'll be fine. I could use a good walk and get a chance to see the neighborhood."

He didn't look convinced and gave a slight shrug. He came from behind the desk with the intention of walking with her outside and pointing her in the right direction, just as the elevator bell tinged and Graham stepped off. His dark eyes widened. A half smile teased his mouth as he approached the desk.

"Everything okay with your flat?"

Flat. That made her smile. "Fine. Everything is great. I was asking Milton about the supermarkets in the area. I want to pick up a few things."

Graham placed the linen laundry bag with the building's logo on the desk. "Can you send these out for me? The usual. Light starch on the shirts."

"Sure thing, Mr. Stone."

"If you don't mind some company, I'll walk with you," Graham offered.

"Great."

Graham extended his arm toward the front door.

* * *

The early-evening weather was still warm. Couples walked hand in hand and families strolled along the avenues pushing baby strollers, while others jogged to the rhythm of the tunes coming from their headsets and earbuds. The towering trees had begun to bloom, filling the air with the sweet scent of awakening.

"Great neighborhood," Alexis said as they made the turn onto First Avenue.

"Yes, it is."

She tilted her head to look at him. "You don't sound convinced."

He laughed lightly. "Oh, I'm convinced." His eyes quickly roamed the street. "Who wouldn't be?"

Alexis studied his profile for a moment, watching his countenance stiffen then relax as if he'd seen something he wished he hadn't.

Graham pushed out a breath and turned his mega-watt smile on her just as they approached Gristedes. He pulled open the heavy glass-and-chrome door. Alexis walked in ahead of him. Every aisle was lined with shoppers and the incredible assortment of goods was beyond imagination. It was a food lovers paradise.

"Take as much time as you need," Graham said. "I have a few things to pick up myself and we can share a cab back."

"Great. Thanks."

"I'll meet you up front when you're done."

She nodded in agreement, grabbed a shopping cart and started off. She probably should have eaten a full meal before setting foot in this emporium. She was tempted to purchase everything that she laid her eyes on and wished she'd brought a list. She selected a case of imported water, fresh vegetables and baked bread, fish, chicken and seasonings, sorbet, yogurt, fruit and mixings for salads. She could easily spend the day here, but her cart was nearly full. She pushed her cart to the checkout line and watched the numbers add up. New York prices were enough to send her into a sticker shock.

Alexis took out her credit card and reluctantly swiped it. *Good thing this job pays well.* She watched the groceries being bagged. Graham was standing at the store's exit talking on his phone when she pushed her loaded cart next to him.

His eyes skipped over her purchases and hers were agape at his. He had two carts filled to the rim and she could only conclude that he hadn't shopped in months.

Graham ended his call. "Get everything you need?"

"I sure hope so." She lifted her chin in the direction of his carts. "I see you must have gotten one of everything."

His eyes crinkled in the corners. "A few things." He stepped away toward a cab that was lined up at the curb. The driver got out and opened the trunk.

"You think there will be enough room?" Alexis asked with a laugh.

"We'll make it fit. Won't we?"

Her eyes leaped to his face, but he was concentrating on getting the bags into the trunk. The muscles of his arms and back flexed as he lifted and deposited each sack. A lick of heat flamed in the center of her stomach. She swallowed.

"All in," he said, turning toward her with a glimmer in his eyes. "Off we go, eh?" He shut the trunk and opened the cab door for her. Alexis slid in and moved over to make room for Graham.

Gone was the scent of his enticing cologne. It was replaced with a cool water fragrance that was even more alluring in its subtlety. She licked her lips.

"Liking the flat so far?"

She blinked rapidly and focused on him. "It's fabulous. More than I could have ever imagined. I can't thank you enough for arranging it."

"You do a good job for R.E.A.L. and that will be thanks enough." He smiled ever so slightly.

Alexis linked her fingers together on her lap while her gaze flicked across his face.

Within moments the taxi was pulling up in front of their building. Glen hurried toward the cab with a luggage cart and helped to unload the bags of groceries and wheeled them inside.

"Don't know whose is whose," Alexis said.

"We can sort it all out upstairs."

They followed Glen onto the elevator. "Where to first?"

"Stop by my flat first, then you can help Ms. Montgomery."

"Sure thing, Mr. Stone."

They rode the elevator to Graham's floor while Glen whistled some off-tune melody. Exiting, Alexis followed the two men down the hall to Graham's apartment. He opened the door. Alexis lingered at the threshold.

"Come on in. You can help sort through."

Alexis came in and looked around. The set up was similar to hers but the decor was decidedly different. Graham's furnishings were in a deep chocolate. A leather sectional that could easily seat ten dominated the living space. At least she thought it did until her gaze landed on the mammoth television. She held back a laugh. *Boys and their toys*. One wall was covered from floor to ceiling with a bookcase that held at least two hundred books. *Impressive.* She wondered if he'd read them all. The tabletops held framed photos of Graham in a variety of situations. Most were with people who she believed were students, in others he was at banquets, and there were several with senators and one with President Obama.

Graham and Glen sifted through the bags and deposited all that belonged to Graham on the kitchen floor and on the counters.

"All done," Graham announced by the time Alexis made her way to the unloading zone. "Glen will take yours down to your place."

"Thanks. When did you get to meet with the president?" she asked while Glen wheeled her groceries to the door.

"I was on his education committee during his first term. That particular photo was taken during a fund-raising dinner for his second term."

"You travel in pretty high circles. I had no idea you were part of the education committee."

"It's not something that I broadcast."

"Why not during his second term?"

"As much as I wanted to help President Obama further his agenda, it took me away from mine. My focus needed to return to R.E.A.L."

She nodded her head in understanding. "Good choice."

He grinned. "I'm glad you think so."

"Good night."

"Good night."

Graham stood in his doorway and waited until the elevator door swished closed. He slowly shut his door and hoped that he hadn't made an awful mistake in hiring Alexis Montgomery.

Alexis had finished putting away her groceries, seasoned a piece of salmon and was waiting for it to finish broiling when her doorbell chimed. She frowned, wiped her hands on a towel and went to the door and pulled it open.

"Graham. Mr. Stone."

"Graham is fine." He held up one of the Gristedes bags. "This was mixed in with mine." He extended the bag that was filled with salad greens.

"I thought it might be with your things. Thank you. I could have come up and gotten it."

"Not a problem. Mmm, something smells good."

"I have some salmon broiling." She paused. "You're welcome to join me if you want. There's plenty."

"Thank you but I'd probably fall asleep. Jet lag is beginning to catch up with me."

She wanted to run her fingers across the expanse of his chest…just to see if it was as hard as she imagined. She smiled instead. "I totally understand. Get some rest." She took the bag. "Thanks."

"Enjoy the rest of your weekend."

"You, too."

Alexis slowly closed her apartment door then rested her head against it and shut her eyes. They were going to wind up in bed together, and there was nothing that either of them could do about it. That she knew for sure. What she didn't know was if she'd be able to keep her job the morning after.

Chapter 4

"Finer than Ian?" Naomi squeaked in disbelief.

"Yes. They haven't invented the word to describe the man." Alexis put her feet up on the couch and snuggled into girl-talk mode. She reached for her glass of wine and took a sip.

"Details, details. Let me live vicariously."

Alexis giggled and then began to fill Naomi in from the moment they met in the car to his dropping off her misplaced groceries.

"Sounds yummy, and a Brit accent, too. Got a little Idris Elba thing going on. Is he single? No, forget that question. You know that mixing business with pleasure is always a disaster."

Alexis sighed. "I know. Bad business for all concerned. Great if it works, a nightmare when it doesn't." She finished off her wine. "But a girl can dream."

"Make sure it's *only* a dream, Lexi," Naomi warned. "This is a phenomenal career move for you, don't sabotage it. Besides, if he is as fine as you say he is, then he probably has a string of women nipping at his heels anyway."

"You're probably right. But I still have my dreams," she said on a playful note. Naomi had always been the more provincial, live by the rules, don't rock the boat kind of girl. She was her conscience, and Alexis knew in the months to come that she was going to need Naomi's good sense to whisper in her ear when it came to Graham Stone.

At eight forty-five on Monday morning, Alexis walked through the doors of R.E.A.L. The offices were located on the fifteenth and sixteenth floors of what was once part of the ABC Television offices on Avenue of the Americas and Fifty-Third Street in Manhattan. Everything looked pretty much the way she remembered from her last visit.

The receptionist looked up from her computer screen and smiled. "Good morning, how can I help you?"

"Good morning. I'm Alexis Montgomery. I start work today."

The young woman's eyes widened. "Oh, Ms. Montgomery." She hopped up from her seat. She extended her hand across the horseshoe shaped desk, which Alexis shook. "Mr. Stone told me to send you straight to his office when you arrived."

Alexis's pulse quickened at the mention of his name. "Certainly."

"Let me advise him that you're here." She quickly pressed a button on the multiline phone and spoke into her headset. "Yes. Of course." She looked across the desk at Alexis. "Straight down the hall, make the first right and his office is on the left."

"Thank you."

Alexis followed the directions and passed several employees in the hallway and others who were getting settled into their offices. She made the turn and slowed her step. The door was partially open. She could hear his distinctive voice but couldn't make out the words. Alexis approached the door and knocked.

"Yes. Come in."

Alexis pushed the door open and stepped inside. Graham stood up from behind his desk. A stunning woman with large, luminous dark eyes and a short pixie haircut turned from her seat to look at Alexis from over her shoulder. She had on a soft pink skirt suit. Everyone couldn't get away with wearing pink without looking like Barbie. But this woman could.

Graham came from around the rather large desk. "Alexis. Good morning." He turned to the seated woman. "Tracy Carter, this is Alexis Montgomery."

Tracy extended her hand but didn't get up. "I've heard a great deal about you."

Alexis shook her proffered hand and was drawn to Tracy's green eyes that reflected like hidden jewels against her sandy-brown complexion. "Nice to meet you."

Tracy's softly tinted lips barely lifted into a smile. "Welcome aboard."

The two women held each other's gaze. Tracy was the first to turn away.

"Tracy is my executive director and probably knows more about how this business runs than I do. She'll bring you up to speed and get you set up in your office." His phone rang. He reached for the phone and gave them a brief look that the meeting was over.

Tracy retrieved her iPad from the desk and stood. "I'll direct you to your office," she said, swinging past Alexis. Alexis offered Graham a tight smile that he completely missed before leaving with Tracy.

"So how long have you been with the organization?" Alexis asked while they walked down the hall and back to the elevators.

Tracy tucked her iPad under her left arm and pressed the up button on the panel. "Since we opened," she said without any further elaboration.

Alexis's right brow flickered upward. She slid a look at Tracy from the corner of her eye. *This was going to be interesting.*

They got off on the sixteenth floor and Tracy silently led the way to the corner office at the end of the wide hallway. She took out a key card from the pocket of her jacket and slid it through the slot like a hotel room. The lock clicked open. Tracy opened the door and stood aside to let Alexis go in. Her first gracious overture since they met.

Alexis looked around. A genuine corner office. Wow. She turned to Tracy. "Thank you."

"IT will be up in about—" she checked her watch "—twenty minutes to get your computer set up, and give you a company cell and iPad. I'll send in Claire. She'll be your assistant. Graham... Mr. Stone has you on his schedule for eleven-thirty in his office."

"Thank you, Tracy."

"I'll send Claire right in." She handed Alexis the key card, walked out and closed the door behind her.

Alexis stared at the door for a moment. Tracy Carter clearly had a bug up her behind. Alexis wasn't quite sure how she fit into the equation but she wasn't going to let Tracy's cold shoulder rub off on her. She walked to the window that overlooked the city. In the distance she could see the treetops of Central Park, and felt the buzz and electricity of the city speeding by below. It was like looking at a magnificent movie with the sound muted.

Her heartbeat escalated. She was here—New York City, with a six-figure job and an apartment on Sutton Place. She had the opportunity to make major changes in education on a global scale. It was everything she could possibly hope for. And then, of course, there was the Graham Stone factor that made the package perfect.

She turned away from the window at the sound of a knock on the door.

"Yes, come in."

The door eased open and a young woman peeked her head in.

"Claire?"

"Yes."

Alexis crossed the room as she spoke. "Please come in."

Claire stepped fully inside. "Good morning, Ms. Montgomery. Claire Davis."

Alexis extended her hand. "My pleasure. I understand we'll be working together."

"Yes, ma'am. Whatever you need."

"How long have you been working here, Claire?"

"Two years."

Alexis bobbed her head. "Good." She blew out a breath. "IT will be up shortly. But until they get here why don't you give me your perspective of R.E.A.L., the who's who and where you see yourself in five years."

Claire blinked back her surprise. "Well…"

Alexis sat down on one of the club chairs and indicated that Claire should sit, as well.

"Before you say anything, I want you to understand that as my assistant I will be entrusting you with keeping me on task, from something as simple as taking a phone message to scheduling appointments, maintaining my calendar, navigating me through the minefield of R.E.A.L. We are a team. That means we work together as a unit. I depend on you and you depend on me to help you do your job. When I'm lagging, I want you to let me know. I can be demanding and get an awful case of tunnel vision when I'm immersed in a project. I give one hundred fifty percent, and I expect no less from anyone that I work with. I make sure that hard work is rewarded."

Claire sat up straighter in her seat. "As I said, I've been here for two years. I worked for Mr. Martin. He had the position before you arrived." She paused a moment. "Actually, we all thought that this position would go to Tracy."

That explained the attitude. Alexis nodded and let Claire continue.

"I have a master's degree in educational leadership. I spent four years with Teach America, teaching fifth grade in Bedford-Stuyvesant in Brooklyn. I'm good at what I do. I'm married and have a two-year-old son. I'm dedicated to my job but I will be honest, my family comes first."

Alexis smiled. "That was the most impressive thing you said…about your family." That little ache that echoed in her belly was still there, not as powerful or as painful as when her mom first passed away, but there nonetheless. She knew the importance of family. She was sure that if her mom would have still been here she would have never left Atlanta, no matter how good this deal was. She cleared her throat. "I think we're going to make a formidable pair."

Claire smiled and appeared to physically relax.

The knock diverted their attention.

"IT," a voice announced.

"Come in," Alexis said, standing. Claire followed suit.

"Morning, I'm Jason. I'm gonna connect all of your equipment and set up your accounts."

"I'll get out of your way."

"It should only take about fifteen minutes." He sat down at the desk, booted up his laptop and turned on her computer. He got set up and went to work.

"Where can I get a cup of coffee?" Alexis asked.

"Come on, I'll show you the employee lounge and my office…and," she added with a grin, "the ladies room."

By the time Alexis and Claire returned to her office, Jason was just finishing up. He showed Alexis how to sign into her email account, and had her sign for an iPad and a company cell phone.

"Thanks, Jason."

"Sure thing. Any problems or questions, we're at extension 2100."

Alexis and Claire sat down to finish their coffee.

"While you're at the meeting with Mr. Stone, I'll get your files set up on your computer and check your supplies to see what you may need."

"Perfect."

Claire got up. "If you need anything before your meeting, I'm on speed dial."

Alexis grinned. "That's definitely good to know."

"And I'll email you my cell so that you can program it into your phone," she added on her way out of the door.

Claire quietly shut the door and Alexis released a long breath. The combination of excitement and nerves ran rampant through her veins. She was eager to get started. She'd had the opportunity to review Graham's plan and she had some ideas on how to make it happen, as well as a suggestion that she hoped he'd agree to. After studying the company's objectives and their projects already in operation, she found one area that had been overlooked and if implemented could elevate R.E.A.L. on yet another level.

She turned on her computer and took her jump drive from her purse and popped it into the computer's USB port. Once the notes that she'd made appeared on her computer screen she reviewed them, made a few corrections and additions and then sent them to a secure folder. Just to be on the safe side, she printed two copies of her report.

She jumped at the sudden ring of her desk phone. She picked it up. Claire was calling to inform her that Mr. Stone wanted to move up their meeting to "right now." She added that it was something she would have to get used to as he often changed meeting times when he was juggling several projects.

"Thanks. I'm on my way." She collected her notes, laptop and cell and took the elevator down. It occurred to her as she stepped off that it was odd that Graham, as the founder and CEO, should be on the lower floor.

But from everything that she'd gleaned about Graham Stone he was anything but status quo.

Alexis took a moment to get her bearings. She caught a glimpse of soft pink at the end of the corridor, moments before the slender figure crossed a threshold and was out of view. She wondered if Tracy would be attending the meeting. Hopefully she would. It would give Alexis an opportunity to see up close and quickly how Tracy operated and the dynamics between Tracy and Graham.

The rhythmic click of her long-legged stride was absorbed in the dove-gray carpet. Graham's door was open. Several people were in the office. She walked in.

Graham sensed her before he actually saw her. The short hairs on the back of his neck tingled. He turned from the conversation he was in with one of his staff members and his gaze zeroed in on Alexis. The tingling sensation spread down the center of his spine. His jaw clenched.

"Ms. Montgomery, please come in." Graham waved her in and the other four people in the room stopped in midsentence and looked at her.

Alexis felt like she was on the runway at Fashion Week and was being appraised by potential buyers. Graham made the introductions.

"All of you are aware that R.E.A.L. has a new VP of Development. I would like to formerly introduce Alexis Montgomery."

Alexis's gaze swept the small assembly and graced them with a warm but professional smile. "Good morning."

Graham continued the introductions that included Anthony Harrelson, Vivian Small, Kwame Knight and

Jae Jennings. They were all the heads of each of the departments: Finance, Corporate Communications, Marketing and Social Media. They would all report to Alexis.

"It's a pleasure to meet all of you. I'm looking forward to us working together and me getting to know you."

"You can set up your individual meetings with the department heads and they can bring you up to speed," Graham said with a briskness that indicated this would not be the place for chitchat and small talk. Everyone took their cue and moved to the rectangular conference table and sat down.

Graham undid the single button on his suit jacket before he took his seat at the head of the table. Alexis found herself between Jae and Vivian. Jae was head of Social Media, and Alexis was sure the evolving digital platforms kept her challenged. She reminded Alexis of a lightning bug in a bottle, buzzing and flashing pinpoints of light and biding its time until the lid was opened and it could escape. Vivian was the diametric opposite. There was a calming aura about her. The strands of silver that ran through her intricately twisted upswept locks belied the buttery smoothness of her skin. Alexis placed the head of Corporate Communications in her early to mid-forties, and noted she wore a striking wedding band encrusted with diamonds.

Anthony Harrelson and Kwame Knight, heads of Finance and Marketing respectively, sat on the opposite side of the table. They could have easily stood in for magazine cover models—gorgeous from head to toe. Alexis absently wondered if good looks was part of the hiring criteria.

Then much to Alexis's surprise Tracy strutted in and joined them, taking the seat nearest Graham.

"Let's begin," Graham said, turning to Tracy.

"The first agenda item is from Finance." She gave a short nod to Anthony and placed her iPad on the table. She took notes as each executive outlined issues of concern in their departments and gave updates on pending projects.

Alexis remained an observer, which allowed her to get a good sense of the staff members' styles and personalities, as well as the dynamic between Graham and Tracy.

It was clear that he relied on her and she knew it. Alexis had to give Tracy her props, though. She knew her stuff. She was up on every nuance in every department and if she didn't understand what was being conveyed, she had no problem challenging the information.

Alexis was surprised at how laid-back Graham appeared to be. She perceived him to be one who relished control, but what she slowly realized was that Graham controlled everyone in the room without uttering a word. It was in a look, a subtle shift of his body in his seat, the sound of a low hum in his throat. Each person in that room deferred and hitched their star to Graham Stone.

The meeting lasted for exactly forty-five minutes. Tracy announced that everyone would have the details of the meeting uploaded to the corporate shared drive by the end of the day.

Everyone except for Tracy and Graham gravitated toward Alexis at the conclusion of the meeting, offering warm words of welcome and promises to contact Claire to set up a one-on-one. Even as she shook hands and smiled and nodded, she managed to catch glimpses

of Graham and Tracy nearly head-to-head at the conference table, talking in low whispers.

Alexis was at the door when Graham's voice stopped
her. "Would you wait a few minutes, Alexis? I'd like to
have a word."

Alexis would have sworn on a stack of hotel bibles
that Tracy's perfectly made-up face contorted. But it
happened so quickly. Maybe she was wrong.

"Of course." She moved back into the room.

Tracy took a seat.

Graham's gaze dropped down to her. "No need for
you to stay."

This time Alexis didn't mistake the shift in Tracy's
expression. It was lightning quick but it happened.

Tracy grabbed up her iPad and phone. "Oh, of course.
I have some calls to make. Don't forget about your three
o'clock." She breezed by Alexis as if she didn't exist.

Inwardly Alexis rolled her eyes at Tracy's immature
behavior and took a seat at the table.

"How has the morning been so far?"

Alexis smiled. "A whirlwind. But not more than I expected. Claire is wonderful and everyone seems friendly
and good at their jobs."

Graham nodded while she spoke and Alexis had the
feeling that Graham wasn't really listening, not from
the way he was looking at her. His unfaltering gaze and
the way he would periodically run his tongue across his
bottom lip ignited a slow heat inside her belly, akin to a
pot of water put on the stove to simmer.

"I'd like to hear your thoughts on the proposal that I
gave you to read."

Alexis swallowed and shifted a bit in her seat. She

crossed her legs. Graham's gaze momentarily tracked the movement then returned to her face.

"The proposal is solid, which I'm sure you already know. I did a bit of research and I couldn't find any other urban model that resembled it. I know we can sell the idea to charter and independent schools."

"I want to begin with the public school system."

Alexis's brow flicked. "Okay. If we select a school and set up a model…"

Graham slowly rocked his jaw and pressed his body forward. "My goal is to give every inner-city child—particularly children of color—the educational opportunities that the kids Uptown and in suburbia get. The Public-Private Partnership Initiative will bring in successful people from every area of discipline to conduct classes on how they did it. Ten months of school, ten separate sessions. We work it into the curriculum."

She was mesmerized by his intensity. The way he presented the proposal was so definitive, so clear, so doable. Except she knew the NYC Department of Education was a sea of bureaucratic red tape. It might take her the length of her five-year contract to pull it off.

"I'll get working on making the contacts at DOE. I take it you have a list of investors."

"I do. I'll get you the list. I want you out front on this." He leaned back a bit the heat that he emanated lessened. His eyes moved lazily across her face. "You'll need to set up individual meetings with each of the potential investors, pitch them the idea, and get them on board. Once you and I knock out all the details—this will be tight," he added, tapping his long finger on the table. "And then we'll have Legal draft a contract for the investors. I need you to complete this phase of the project in three days."

Alexis nodded. "I'll get right on it." *Right on it. I wonder how that would feel?*

The corner of his mouth curved ever so slightly as if he'd read her wicked little thoughts. Her face heated.

She stood and smoothed her skirt. "If there's nothing else…"

"I'd like us to meet again on Thursday to discuss your progress. I have to go out of town on Friday."

"Oh." A twinge of disappointment pinched her. "Of course. I'll get as much done as I can."

"All of the organization's resources are at your disposal. All of the department heads report to you. Don't hesitate to use them."

"Yes, thank you." She walked to the door.

"Enjoy the rest of your day," Graham said.

The murmur of his voice slid up her spine and tickled the hairs at the nape of her neck and the tiniest of moans escaped from her lips. She glanced over her shoulder. "You, too."

Alexis headed back to her office, acutely aware of the dampness between her legs. Was she going to have to carry around an extra pair of panties in order to be in the same room with Graham? Damn.

The best thing to get her mind and body off of him was work and she had plenty of it. Yet, even as she returned to her corner office she wondered what was going to be more challenging; completing the details of his complex proposal in three days or staying in her right mind around him.

Chapter 5

Graham loosened his tie and slowly lowered himself into his high-backed leather chair. Her scent still lingered in the air. It was on his fingertips even though he hadn't touched her, didn't dare. He was beginning to believe that it was some kind of aromatic hallucination because he inhaled her in his apartment, in his sheets, in the shower, in the car. It was as if he'd absorbed her into his pores. An image of her sitting in front of him flashed. His cock jumped in response.

His jaw clenched. Alexis was a distraction. And he didn't like distractions. It was good that he was getting away. The trip would give him some time and space to clear his head and shake himself back to reality. He may have made a mistake taking her on. Had he met with her in person prior to the hire, this spot of trouble could have been avoided. But she'd signed a contract that he had countersigned. To break it would be a public relations nightmare. Not to mention the cost and legal ramifications. He'd have to show cause. And getting a hard-on when she was anywhere near him was not a reason. He would have to get her to demonstrate her inability to perform the job she was hired to do.

At least that much was in place. It would be a challenge for her to complete the initial assignment he'd given her in three days. He pursed his lips and thoughtfully rubbed his chin. He'd start there.

Alexis called Claire's phone and asked her to put together the list of DOE contacts that had been used in the past. Maybe she would recognize a name or two from the zillion educational conferences that she'd attended over the years. She also asked Claire for a list of any outside consultants that had gone into any of the schools that R.E.A.L. dealt with.

"Not a problem. I'll start on the lists right away. Oh, did you want to order lunch or will you be going out?"

"Hmm, I hadn't really thought about it, but maybe I'll go out and get a feel for things."

"There are some great places one block up on Seventh Avenue and if you walk down toward Radio City Music Hall, go down the stairs of the McGraw Hill Building, there are some really good restaurants there as well."

"Great. Thanks." She disconnected the call and turned her full attention to the proposal in its entirety, then began to break it down into manageable parts and then started rewriting, expanding some sections and compressing others.

As she worked it was as if she was inside Graham's head, thinking how he thought, seeing what he saw, want-

ing what he wanted. She worked with a single purpose to
please him—with the final product. Although it was work
there was an almost sensual quality to it that stirred her.
To Alexis there was nothing more sensually stimulating
than getting inside someone's head—becoming one with
them—a mental symbiosis. Her nipples tingled inside her
lace push-up bra. She gave her head a shake and willed
her senses to dispel their fix on Graham.

She drew in a long breath of resolve, rolled her shoulders and targeted all of her concentration on the task
at hand.

Alexis glanced up to see Claire walking into her office. She had a folder in her hand. Alexis pushed back
from the desk and noticed the time on her computer.
She'd been working for nearly two hours straight. It was
almost three o'clock.

"You need to take a break," Claire said.

Alexis stretched her arms above her head and her tight
body sighed in relief. "You're right and I'm starved."

"Do you still want to go out or would you rather
order?"

"Hmm, I think I'll order. Touring will have to wait
for another day. Do you have any menus?"

"Sure do. I'll be right back."

While Claire went for the menus, Alexis did an as-
sessment of what she had accomplished. She broke the
project down into six steps each with its own compo-
nents and time frames. During the time she had her nose
to the grindstone, Claire had prepared the last of the contacts and uploaded them to the shared drive. She opened
the file and scanned the individual names and organi-

zations and was mildly disappointed that there weren't any names that she was acquainted with.

Claire returned with the menus, a veritable Who's Who of dining.

"Wow," Alexis said on a breath, as she flipped through the stack. "Any recommendations?"

"Roof, if you like Thai." She plucked a menu from the stack.

"Sounds fine."

"I can order for you."

"Would you? Some kind of rice and chicken."

Claire grinned. "Okay. Anything else?"

"Some green tea."

"Hot or cold?"

"Hot."

"You got it. Give them about twenty minutes."

"Thanks."

Claire walked out to her desk to call. Alexis pulled herself up, stretched and walked to the window. The first full day in New York City was almost behind her. She felt a sliver of accomplishment. Yet, looking down on the rushing world below she knew she was only a minor player on the New York stage.

"How was your day so far?" Alexis spun around.

"Mr. Stone."

"Graham. Please." He walked into her office. "Getting settled?"

"Yes," she said on a breath. She sat behind her desk. "Claire is the best."

His eyes said he agreed. "I won't keep you." He slid a hand into his pocket. "Remember, everyone is at your disposal, eh?"

Including you? "I'll remember. Thanks for stopping by," she said to his back.

Claire and Graham passed each other in the doorway. She had Alexis's lunch and placed it on the desk. As hungry as Alexis was, she would first have to calm her jangling nerves following Graham's impromptu visit.

After a few minutes, Alexis opened the bag containing her food and peered into one of the cartons. She tasted a spoonful of the delicious stir-fry rice, then noticed that her green tea was missing. Her forehead pinched in annoyance. She returned the carton to the bag, grabbed her purse and walked out. She stopped at Claire's desk.

"Everything okay?"

"Yes, fine. But they forgot the tea."

"Oh, I'm sorry. I'll call them."

Alexis waved away the offer. "No worries. I could use a walk. I'll be back shortly."

She stepped outside into the late-afternoon sun and was assaulted by the noise, the rush of people, and the aromas from the food vendors. She stepped off the Plaza platform and down the three steps to the sidewalk. People were everywhere. She looked left then right trying to decide which way to walk when she noticed a flash of soft pink across the street.

Her gaze followed Tracy as she approached the entrance of the Hilton Hotel and was met by Graham.

Chapter 6

Alexis stood transfixed as she watched them walk in together. *What in the hell? Graham and Tracy?* She thought Tracy's attitude was because of the job, but clearly it went much deeper. He probably didn't give Tracy her job so as not to show favoritism to the woman he was sleeping with.

She wanted to hurl something. Instead she spun around, tea forgotten, and turned back inside. The truth was she had no claims on the man. He was her boss and she didn't cross that line anyway. So why was she so pissed? She repeatedly stabbed the elevator button while tapping her foot in fury. The person she was really angry with was herself for getting her panties in a bunch in the first place.

The elevator arrived. She had four years and three-hundred and sixty-four days left on a contract. She certainly couldn't spend her time worrying or thinking about Graham Stone—who'd already sunk in her estimation.

"Got your tea?" Claire asked as Alexis breezed by her desk.

"No. Changed my mind."

Graham stepped out of the shower and wrapped a towel around his waist. Steam clouded the mirror and swirled around the room like a foggy morning on the English moors.

He wiped off a spot on the glass and peered closer. He needed a shave. It could wait until the morning.

He entered his adjoining bedroom, picked up the remote from the table and turned to the game. Playoff season—forty games, forty nights. Tonight Brooklyn Nets played the Miami Heat. He didn't really care who was playing, all he wanted to do was lose himself in something other than thinking about Alexis.

After leaving the hotel, he decided to come home instead of returning to the office and possibly seeking out Alexis again. He certainly couldn't keep too much distance, but at least they were on different floors. But she was constantly on his mind. Like now. Was she home yet? Had she gotten out of her clothes? What did she wear beneath those formfitting suits? Did she—

His cell phone buzzed, snapping him back to reality. He picked the phone up from the nightstand. Blake's name was illuminated on the face of the phone.

"Hey, brother."

"What's up man?" Blake responded.

Blake Stevens was Graham's closest friend, more like the brother he never had. They'd met on a flight to

Los Angeles years ago to see the Lakers game. It was a friendship made in sports heaven. Their love of the game was only eclipsed by their passion for their work and their loyalty toward each other.

"Just getting in. Relaxing. Plan to watch the game."

"That's why I'm calling, bro. I just snagged two floor seat tickets for tonight's game at the Barclays."

"What!" Graham grinned like a kid.

"I'm serious. Can you meet me in Brooklyn by seven-thiry? Tip-off is at eight."

"You don't have to ask me twice. Getting ready as we speak."

"Cool. I'll meet you out front on the Atlantic Avenue side."

"See you there."

Graham tossed the phone on the bed and hurried to his walk-in closet. Jeans, cotton shirt, jacket, sneakers—that would be the outfit of choice for tonight.

This was what he needed, a night out with his mate enjoying their favorite sport; the perfect anecdote for his crazy fix on Alexis.

He called down to the front desk and asked Milton to have his car pulled out front. After a few last-minute checks for house keys, phone, wallet, he walked out snatching up his cap on the way. He pulled the bill low over his brow while he waited for the elevator. The door opened and he stepped on humming to himself. Moments later the door opened and Alexis stood in front of him.

For an instant she froze then stepped on just before the doors closed.

"Evening," he said.

"Hi." She forced a smile. The memory of seeing him and Tracy walking into the hotel together bloomed afresh.

"How was your first day?"

"Busy." She tried to stay focused on the elevator doors but she couldn't ignore the heat that radiated from him or his scent that clouded her thoughts.

Graham frowned. She was different somehow. Distant. Chilly even. "Heading out?"

She barely glanced at him. She didn't dare or she might forget why she was so pissed. "Going for a run. You?"

He grinned at her and her heart tumbled in her chest. "After the day I had with the last-minute request to give an impromptu presentation at a business meeting at the Hilton today, I'm ready for some R & R."

Alexis's thoughts flashed back to earlier in the day. *A meeting.* She felt utterly ridiculous for having imagined the worst.

"My mate—friend—got two floor seats to the Miami Heat and the Brooklyn Nets game at the Barclays Center," he was saying

Her brown eyes widened. "Really? Floor seats! That…"

He chuckled. "I know. Figured I'd be watching the game on television. Don't tell me you're a basketball fan."

She dropped her hand on her hip and looked up at him with a smirk. "Don't get me started with b-ball. I've been a fan since grade school. Played during high school, too."

"You played?" He wondered what she would look

like all hot and sweaty running up and down the court
in shorts.

The bell pinged and the doors swished open.

"Now I'm impressed," he teased.

Alexis laughed. "Enjoy the game." She walked out
ahead of him, pushed through the front door and was
gone.

Graham stopped at the front desk, retrieved his car
keys from Milton and walked out to get in his car. He
caught a glimpse of Alexis an instant before she turned
the corner.

He got in behind the wheel. *She likes basketball.*
Maybe they could watch a game together sometime.
Not a good idea. He pulled off into traffic. Not a good
idea at all.

After the game Graham and Blake stopped in Jay-
Z's 40/40 Club in the Barclays Center for a late dinner.
They sat at the bar and recapped the game, drinking beer
and eating peanuts until the waitress arrived and told
them that the table was ready. They placed their dinner
orders and watched ESPN on the restaurant television.

"So did the new VP start? Alexis something, right?"

"Yeah, started today."

"So, what's she like in person?"

The center of his chest grew warm. His lips quirked.
"Smart, professional." *Sexy, throaty voice, sensual scent.*

Blake watched the expressions play across Graham's
face. "And she lives in your building *and* you work together." He paused a beat. "I've seen that look before, G."

"What look?"

"You know. The *I'm interested* look."

"Can't happen."

"Can't or won't?"

"Same thing."

"There hasn't been anyone serious in your life in forever. You always get involved with women that you know the relationship won't go anywhere. Sounds like you're heading down the same road again."

Graham glanced up. He couldn't argue. Blake was right. The only women who appealed to him were women who were unattainable. That way he could remain uncommitted—until the interest waned. The intrigue was the challenge. When he conquered the challenge he lost interest. But he continued to try to find someone to fill the spaces that the last person left. There was always a constant, aching emptiness inside of him, an emptiness that he filled with things, and bodies and work; not necessarily in that order.

Graham shook his head. "Not this time. She's an employee. I can't cross that line."

Blake looked his friend in the eye. "Then there's no problem."

"Right, no problem."

Alexis arrived early the following morning, wanting to get a jump start on the list. Her goal was to sequester herself in her office and work the phones. She wanted to provide Graham with the list of people from DOE that were willing to discuss the plan and potential investors that were willing to come on board.

She planned to approach the investors first. She figured if she could offer up some well-known names to the DOE, they would be more willing to play ball.

All of the offices were still empty. It was barely 7:00 a.m. She switched on the lights in the office, closed her door and turned on her computer. It was much too early to make calls, but she wanted to finish fleshing out some of the details. Although Graham said that all of the departments were at her disposal, she wanted to secure the foundation before she brought anyone in.

She set her mug of coffee on the desk, took the satin bag from her purse and put it in the bottom desk drawer.

There was a noise. Her head snapped up. The door inched open. She drew in a breath and reached for the phone. The door pushed all the way open. Graham stood in the threshold.

"Dammit, you scared me," she said on a shuddering breath.

"Sorry. No one is usually here at this hour. I saw the light on."

She tossed her head and willed her heart to slow. For a moment she saw her story being aired on *The First 48 Hours*, "Education Executive Found Strangled in Her Midtown Office." What was equally as crazy was her reprimanding the owner of the company for checking on his offices. "Are you usually here this early?" she asked, instead of apologizing.

"Usually." He took a few steps inside. "Why so early for you?" He approached her desk.

Her body tensed. "A lot to do. The clock is ticking. The one you set, remember?"

He almost smiled.

"How did you enjoy the game?"

"Great. Good time."

His smile was infectious and her own body loosened. "I haven't been to a live game in a while. I used to go to the Hawks games when I could."

"Maybe...next time...if I get tickets, maybe you'd like to come."

She blinked. "Um, sure." She nodded. "That would be fun."

"I'll let you know—for next time." He moved closer. "What's on your agenda today?"

She gave him a rundown on what her plan was and the preliminary timeline.

Graham didn't really care what she was saying. He only wanted to watch her mouth, catch the sparkle in her eyes and listen to the rhythm of her voice. He had to get out of there.

"I should let you get to it." He backed up then turned toward the door and was gone.

Alone she gave in to the tremors that gently rippled along her spine and up her inner thighs. Her lashes fluttered. Her eyes closed. She could hear her heartbeat. *Four years, three-hundred and sixty-three days.*

She opened her eyes, reached down and pulled open the bottom drawer of her desk and took out the satin pouch that contained her fresh panties. She went to the ladies room to change.

Graham spent the day in meetings, responding to phone calls and putting the final touches on his trip to Washington, D.C. He had a meeting with the secretary of education. He was part of the subcommittee that was working on the Administration's education reform package.

His intention was to present the first draft of his proposal to the secretary. If Alexis was as good as he believed she was, the proposal and all of its moving parts would wind up being a major component of game-changing legislation. But the plan had to be airtight.

Over the next two days Alexis met with the department heads and gave them their instructions. She didn't need final details but she did need preliminaries from Finance and Marketing in particular. She'd come up with a slogan for the project that she hoped Graham would be on board with when they met later that afternoon.

Since the morning that he'd walked in on her she hadn't seen him—not in the office and not at the apartment. Maybe he'd been spending his time on and off the job with Tracy. Every time she thought about the two of them together the pulse in her temples began to pound.

She tried to convince herself that the reason for her anger was because of the inappropriateness of the relationship, and the brazenness of it. The truth was Tracy had him and she didn't. *Get over it, girl.*

Alexis saved the last document and added it to the PowerPoint file. Getting with the boss wasn't why she'd come to New York and joined this organization. That's what she needed to keep at the forefront, not images of Graham's mouth on...

The *tap-tap* on her door jerked her from her mental trip down Graham Stone lane.

"Yes, Claire." She shifted in her seat.

"Mr. Stone said he's ready for you to come down."

"Great. Thanks." She plucked her flash drive from the USB port, checked the hard copies in the file folders and grabbed her phone. She grinned at Claire. "Wish me luck."

Claire smiled broadly. "You don't need luck. You got

this. I've seen how hard you worked since you arrived. It will show."

Alexis drew in the praise. "Thanks. See you soon."

It had been quite some time since she'd had to prove herself on this level. But she was confident that she brought her A-game.

She briefly stopped at Graham's secretary's desk.

"Go right in, Ms. Montgomery. He's expecting you."

"Thank you." She tapped on the door and walked in. Her forward motion halted for a half step when she saw Tracy sitting at the conference table. It was logical that she would be there, but it didn't mean that Alexis had to like it.

Graham stood. He zeroed in on her like a laser beam, his gaze taking in every inch of her.

"Good morning," Alexis said, entering the office in long confident strides. She placed her things on the table and sat.

"Anxious to see what you've managed to put together," Tracy said, her tone a note short of condescending.

Oh, how she wished for a minute that she was a different kind of woman so that she could back slap that smug look off of Tracy's face. She forced a tight smile.

Alexis flipped open the folder and gave Graham the written proposal. "I've prepared a PowerPoint presentation. We can watch it on the big screen." She glanced at Graham.

He lifted his chin toward the projector. "Go right ahead."

Alexis walked over to the end of the office and turned on the system that was tucked away in the wood paneling. She inserted the flash drive, waited for it to register and then scrolled to the PowerPoint icon and clicked.

Alexis had meticulously searched for images that highlighted each of the elements of the presentation; classrooms, urban streets, countless faces of children, teachers, actors, artists, businessmen and -women, college campuses, corporate offices and science labs. In addition to the textual and visual images, she'd incorporated voice narration to guide the viewer through the screens.

Graham was beyond the programs of the past. He wanted to utilize a fresh approach for the educational system. As he watched the presentation, he was struck with the realization that Alexis had found the way to get inside his head, translate his ideas and bring them to reality. It was a turn-on that surprised him. And hearing her voice during the entire presentation only added to his personal pleasure.

The screen faded to black. Alexis turned toward Graham and her insides jumped from the impact of his stare.

"Beyond my expectations."

Alexis smiled. "Thank you."

"I think the section about the class implementation could use some work," Tracy said, the disgust in her voice and on her face barely contained.

Graham slid her a look. "I don't."

Tracy's right cheek twitched.

"It's exactly what I was looking for. You took the idea and made it three-dimensional." He paused. "I'd like you to go with me to Washington to make the presentation."

Tracy actually jumped up. She looked from Graham to Alexis. Her mouth partially opened. "I'll see about getting Ms. Montgomery a ticket," she said, recovering quickly.

"And a room," Graham added.

Alexis was trying to process what had just happened.

Tracy picked up her things from the desk and walked out.

"Can we rewind a bit," Alexis said.

Graham frowned.

"Go back to the part about me going with you to Washington, D.C."

"Yes, I'm taking the train down tonight. I'll be staying at the Marriott. The meeting is scheduled with the Secretary of Education at noon tomorrow."

Alexis pressed her hands against her stomach. "I… I'll need to go home and pack. How long will we be staying?"

"Until Sunday. There's the meeting tomorrow and a brunch with the subcommittee on Saturday. I usually try to take in some of the sights while in town, check out a few shows. You're more than welcome to stay." He saw her get ready to protest. "Actually, I insist."

She stared at him a moment. She couldn't allow her own crazy thoughts to have her making this invitation more than what it was—business.

"It would be too self-serving of me to present this proposal without you there." His gaze moved slowly over her face.

"This is your concept."

"Yes, but you made it real. You can sell it."

She knew she could. There was no doubt in her mind. This was what she'd come to do and she would. "Fine. Not a problem." She pushed back from her seat and stood. "What time?"

"The five-fifty from Penn Station. We should get in about ten."

Alexis nodded. "Should I meet you… Where?"

"The car will pick us up from the apartment at four-thirty."

"I'll be ready."

"Good." He turned away.

She felt as if she'd been suddenly tossed off a tall building. Without his gaze to anchor her she had the sensation of free-falling.

Chapter 7

Alexis hadn't traveled on Amtrak in a number of years. She'd forgotten how much she enjoyed it. It was like taking a mini-adventure. This time, however, the adventure included traveling with a handsome, too-sexy-for-his-own-good man.

As promised, Michael was out front with the car at four-thirty. He strolled over to her and took her bag.

"Good to see you again, Ms. Montgomery."

"Same here, Michael. Is Mr. Stone in the car?"

"Yes, ma'am." He opened the door for her.

At least this time he didn't have the upper hand of surprise. She got in. Graham was on the phone. He nodded in acknowledgment and continued his conversation. Alexis settled herself against the leather.

This car was a Lincoln and not a limo. She had to sit

next to Graham instead of across from him. She didn't
know if that was better or worse.

She kept herself distracted with checking email on
her phone and pretending that the short sparks of electricity that were snapping between them like a summer
lightning storm didn't exist.

"Michael should have us to Penn Station in no time,"
Graham said.

Drawn by the sound of his voice her gaze traveled up
from his thighs, settling for a moment at his midsection,
up to his mouth, and darting away to settle on his eyes
that were cinched at the corners as if he was trying to
peer through her.

She ran her tongue slowly across the bottom lip. His
dark eyes flashed for an instant.

"It's barely been a week and I'm already on my first
trip."

"The first of many when this proposal gets accepted."

"You sound very confident."

"I have every reason to be." His gaze moved over her
face. "You did an amazing job. Tomorrow you will convince the Secretary."

Her expression brightened. "Yes. I will."

The train ride was better than the trips she remembered. Maybe it was the Northeast Corridor route, and
the fact that it was early evening and the sun was lowering itself over the horizon casting an orange glow across
the picturesque landscape that went from towering office
buildings and sprawling bridges to smaller towns and
shimmering lakes. Or perhaps it was the fact that she
was traveling business class for the first time with leg
room and a private dining car. Or maybe it was being in

the company of Graham. He was utterly entertaining and observant and knowledgeable about everyone and everything from sports to politics to religion, to literature and reality television. He had her in stitches talking about the Kardasians and the British equivalent the Bennings.

This was a different Graham Stone. He was relaxed, animated. The intensity and control that he exhibited in the office was gone. She liked this version of him, too.

They had a light meal on the train—cheeseburgers and beer. He promised the next meal they shared would be in a "proper restaurant with proper waiters and good wine."

She laughed. *Next time.* She wouldn't read anything into that. He was only being polite. But she could easily imagine herself sitting at a circular table with white linen and low lights sharing a bottle of wine with Graham.

The nearly four-hour Acela train ride was as much a trip from north to south—crossing the Mason-Dixon Line—as it was an educational excursion into the inner workings of her boss, crossing an invisible line in their relationship.

They exited at Union Station in Washington, D.C., and stepped out into the balmy spring night. The scent of cherry blossoms blended with the engine exhaust. They joined the line for taxis and inched along until it was their turn. The driver got out of the red cab and put their bags in the trunk.

"Where to?"

"The Capitol Marriott. E Street SW."

The cab pulled away from the curb and zipped in and out of the Downtown traffic. Friday night in D.C. was like Friday night in any metropolitan city across the country—busy, lights, cars and bodies. But there was a special rarefied air in D.C. The iconic silhouettes of the Lincoln Memorial, the Capitol building and, of course, the White House gave D.C. the gravitas that no other American city could claim.

They pulled up to the hotel. Graham paid the driver and the bellhop brought their bags inside.

"Graham Stone," he said with that James Bond cool that was such a total turn-on. He should have his own theme music, she thought and giggled inside.

"And you should also have a reservation in the name of Alexis Montgomery."

"Yes, sir." The clerk printed out the room information, swiped his credit card and gave him two sets of room key cards. "You'll both be on the tenth floor, Mr. Stone. Rooms 1012 and 1014."

"Thank you."

"You need help with your luggage?"

Graham looked at Alexis. She shook her head, no. She only had her small overnight bag that she managed to fill with four days worth of clothes. She pulled it behind her as they walked to the bank of elevators.

They exited on the tenth floor and walked down the carpeted hallway to their rooms that faced each other.

Graham inserted the key card in the slot of Alexis's door. The green light flashed. He turned the handle, stepped in first and turned on the light. He took a quick look around the one bedroom suite, opened closets, the bathroom and checked that the phones were working.

Alexis didn't know if she should be flattered that he was being so gallant, or insulted by his presumptuousness to walk into her room uninvited.

"Rest well. If you want to join me for breakfast, I should be down at the hotel dining room by nine-thirty."

"Thank you."

He turned, crossed the room and left.

Alexis walked behind him and locked the door. She moved back to the center of the room and took in the suite in a slow circle.

She had a full-size, contemporarily furnished living room, an efficiency kitchen, bath with a Jacuzzi tub, a separate bedroom complete with a king-size bed and a terrace.

Graham certainly didn't do anything halfway, she mused as she began to strip out of her clothes. She unpacked her toiletries and hung up her clothes in the closet. With every step she took another wave of exhaustion flowed through her. To be on the safe side she called the front desk and asked for a wake-up call for eight.

As she slipped beneath the cool, crisp sheets and sleep began to overtake her, the last clear thought was about sitting at a breakfast table across from Graham. If not a candlelit dinner, breakfast would have to do.

Graham was up by six, down in the hotel gym by six-thirty. He worked out for more than an hour trying to burn off the jumpy energy that had him running his mouth like a horny teenager on the train ride down and kept him up half the night. He wanted to believe that it was the upcoming meeting. He knew better. It wasn't. It was Alexis.

More than once he picked up the phone to call her room. It was only the fact that he was holding on to the fraying threads of common sense that kept him from unraveling their business relationship and dialing her room. Messy. That's all it could be. But the part of him that ached to have her didn't give a damn about messy. He wiped the sweat from his face and draped the towel around his neck.

Would she meet him for breakfast? He stabbed the button for the elevator. The doors swooshed open and Alexis stepped out.

"Oh," she squeaked. Totally taken aback. The doors closed behind her.

He wiped his face again, to cover his delight and his surprise. "Good morning. Had I known that you wanted to use the gym I would have buzzed you and we could have worked out together."

His T-shirt was damp and clinging to his broad chest. His gym shorts hung low on his hips. Perspiration trickled down her spine and she hadn't even set foot in the gym yet. What did he say?

Graham tipped his head to the side and looked down at her. She blinked. "Are you okay?"

"Yes. Fine." She smiled brightly. "I'm sorry. For a minute I thought I might have...left my room key."

"Oh, yes, you'll need it to use the equipment."

Her throat was terribly dry. "So you're all done."

"Early riser. Seems we have quite a few things in common—basketball, education and physical activity."

She coughed. "And I guess I'd better catch up."

"I'll let you get to it. Breakfast, later?"

"Sure. See you then."

He gave her a short nod and stepped onto the elevator.

"How was your workout?" he asked as he finished his cup of coffee.

"Good. I always feel better after running or being

in the gym. Gets the juices flowing." Oh damn, she shouldn't have said that.

He cut into his stack of buttermilk pancakes. "I totally agree." He looked across at her from beneath long silken lashes.

Her stomach flipped then settled. Handling men was as second nature to Alexis as breathing. She was good at it. Damned good at it. She didn't let a man, no matter who he was, get into her head and start stirring up feelings. She'd been down that road and she didn't like it one bit. But this man, he was something else. He was different. He'd somehow gotten into her head. He'd stirred up feelings. And she wanted him like she'd never wanted another man. She wanted him with a hunger that was ravenous. But he was her boss. It didn't matter what she wanted.

"Have you met with the Secretary before?" she asked, needing to turn her thoughts into a more appropriate direction.

He nodded while he chewed and swallowed. "We've met at several events here in D.C. But this will be my first formal meeting with her."

Miranda Velasquez was the first Latina to hold the position. It was believed, in private circles, that because of her background she would have the empathy that was needed to push through changes needed to overhaul the education system and policies that affected inner-city and low-income students. She was tough but fair, having served as a judge in the New York City courts for ten years.

"Oh, so you brought me as back up," she teased.

He chuckled. "Absolutely."

* * *

Alexis took her time getting dressed. She'd selected a teal-blue two-piece skirt suit that was both fashionable and professional. The cut was perfect and she always loved how it fit. The hug of the jacket at the waist, then the soft flare that played a halo around her hips was the highlight of the suit's design.

She checked that she had her iPad and phone. She placed them all in a leather tote that matched her suit. She checked her makeup, added her compact and lipstick into her tote along with her wallet and room key. Took one last look around, did a mental check of everything that she needed and then walked out.

Graham was waiting for her in the lobby and did a double take when he saw her walking toward him. His chest tightened. He slowly stood as she approached. She was stunning. The color was incredible on her. She turned heads and he had the irrational urge to tell those lascivious eyes to back the hell off. She was his. His jaw clenched. She wasn't his and he would have to remember that they were on their way to an important business meeting and not a date.

"Hi. Ready?" She smiled up at him.

"Yes. We can grab a cab out front," he said, his British cool running hot and thick.

She gave him a curious glance. "Are you all right? No last-minute nerves?"

"Not at all." He held the door open for her.

The doorman hailed them a cab.

"Four hundred Maryland Avenue SW," he said through the window. He pulled open the door and helped Alexis into her seat. He got in behind her and stayed close to the window. He needed to get his head in the game.

Alexis adjusted herself in her seat and her skirt inched up. Graham tore his gaze away and stared straight ahead.

They arrived within moments to the building that housed the offices of the Secretary of Education and after signing in, having their IDs checked and their body and possessions scanned, they were admitted and escorted to Secretary Velasquez's office.

After waiting for only a few moments at reception, they were taken into the private conference room. Secretary Velasquez and her under secretary joined them as well as her chief of staff. Following introductions and handshakes, Graham wasted no time in outlining his plan that had the potential to revolutionize the classroom and give inner-city kids the boost that it needed.

The Secretary nodded while Graham spoke and everyone took notes.

"That is the basis of the proposal, Madam Secretary. I'd like to turn over the rest of the presentation to my VP, Ms. Montgomery."

"Thank you." Alexis gave Graham a short nod and the spark in her eyes telegraphed how pleased she was with his delivery. "What I'd like to do now is to present a visual of the program in action—*Innovate to Educate*."

A half hour later the presentation came to a close. The room was momentarily silent.

"You already have agreements with your local DOE and these vendors?"

"Yes," Alexis responded.

"And those are only the ones that we have signed on for the pilot," Graham added.

Velasquez nodded. She leaned over and whispered something to the under secretary. "I like it, Graham. I can't guarantee that we can get it passed on a national level with legislation. There are so many squeaky wheels on this wagon. And the partisanship in Congress has pretty much brought everything to a halt."

"I know, I know," Graham said on a breath. "All across the country public education is under siege, disproportionately effecting urban schools and children of color. You would think that partisanship could be put aside for the good of our children and the country."

"You're preaching to the choir, Graham," she said. "I think the plan is brilliant. It's a no-brainer. But turning it into legislation is an entirely different battle."

"What are the next steps?"

"You have your meeting tomorrow with the education subcommittee. Convince them and it will get you a step closer."

Graham nodded. Velasquez stood. The meeting was over. Graham came around the table to shake her hand. "Thank you for your time, Miranda," he said in an intimate voice.

She covered his hand with both of hers. "Whatever I can do to help, you know I will."

"I appreciate that."

Alexis approached. Miranda released Graham's hand and extended hers to Alexis. "It was a pleasure to meet you. The presentation is a winner."

"Thank you. I'm honored to meet you."

"My staff will keep me posted," she said to Graham. "You know my line is always open for you if you run into any snags." She turned and her entourage followed her out.

Graham faced Alexis and wanted to hug her. Instead he beamed a smile. "You were great."

"I had great material to work with."

He chuckled. "Why don't we take this mutual admiration society out of here."

"You want to go back to the hotel, or do a bit of the tourist thing?" Graham asked once they were outside.

"Did you have some place in mind?"

He slid his hand into his pant pocket, pulled out his cell phone and touched the screen a few times. "We're not far from Constitution Gardens." He glanced up from the info on his screen and was rocked again when their gazes connected.

She gave a playful shrug. "Sure. They have food?" She grinned. "I'm starved."

"I think we can do something about that. This way," he added, placing a hand at the small of her back.

During a lunch of grilled salmon and a mixed green salad they talked about their meeting with the Secretary.

"I think it went off without a hitch," Graham said. "Thanks to you."

"It's a great concept, Graham. The world needs to know about it."

He chuckled. "That's why I have you," he said in a tone that reached down and gently stroked her.

She lifted her water glass to her lips and took a long swallow to cool the flame that flared inside. "So...who do you think is going to win the NBA finals?"

His eyes cinched at the corners as he smiled, then launched into his predicitions.

By the time they returned to the hotel it was nearly five and Alexis was officially tired.

"I think I'm going to take a nap," she said, stifling a yawn when they reached the elevator.

"Sounds like a plan."

The doors opened. They stepped on.

"Speaking of plans, what would you like to do for dinner? Hotel or perhaps somewhere else?"

Her pulse skipped. "The hotel is fine."

"All right then. Seven-thirty?"

"Seven-thirty."

He walked her to her room.

"Are you going to check for the boogeyman again?" she teased.

"For some reason I believe you could manage to even put the boogeyman under your spell."

The air stalled in her chest. Her eyes flew up to his and the ground shifted beneath her, then settled.

"Seven-thirty," he murmured in that cool undertone that inflamed her. He turned around, crossed the hall and entered his room.

Chapter 8

Alexis drew in a long breath and studied herself in the full-length mirror mounted on the bathroom door.

She'd chosen a sleeveless blouse in a white rayon blend and black broomstick palazzo pants with a wide waistband. Her accessories were silver; a cuff bracelet and teardrop earrings.

She checked her watch. It was 7:30 p.m. She didn't want to keep him waiting, but she didn't want to appear overly eager either. She sprayed the space in front of her with her perfume and then stepped into its floating scent.

Since she'd returned to the room she'd been unable to shake his last statement. No matter how hard she tried to spin it, he was coming on to her and she wasn't imagining it. Her insides jumped as she picked up her purse, checked for the essentials and left her bedroom.

* * *

Graham came to the dining room early. He sat at the bar. He needed a drink to smooth him out, massage the rough edges.

Whatever happened tonight during dinner would determine which way the rest of the evening went. He'd already made up his mind that if Alexis gave him the vibes that she wanted more than just dinner, he was ready to push aside company rules and personal ethics.

He finished off a shot of bourbon, turned halfway on the bar stool and everything stood still. Alexis was in the doorway. She hadn't seen him yet and he took that moment to watch her while she was unaware, capture the look of wonder and expectation on her face and imprint it forever in his memory. And then her searching eyes found him. Her eyes brightened and her slow, sensual smile lit up the room.

Graham stood as she walked toward him. Her outfit gave her the illusion of floating across the floor. *A sexy angel.*

"Evening…you look…stunning."

"Thank you," she said, her throaty tone an even lower octave.

"Would you care for a drink first or are you ready… to be seated?"

She placed her purse on the bar. "I think I'd like a drink first. But I'm sure they could bring it to our table."

Graham kept his eyes on her, dazzled by her in a new way, while he signaled for the bartender.

"What can I get you?" The bartender looked from one to the other.

"I'd like an apple martini," Alexis said.

"Refill on the bourbon."

"Coming right up."

When the bartender returned with their drinks, Graham let him know that they were ready to be seated. Shortly the hostess approached and took them to their table. It was tucked away from the front and off the path of foot traffic. It was about as private as it could get for a hotel restaurant that didn't require special reservations.

Graham held Alexis's chair while she sat down.

Alexis took in her surroundings. "Nice. Different ambiance at night."

"Yes, very," he said, watching her over the rim of his glass.

Alexis lifted her glass and brought it delicately to her lips and briefly wondered if it would happen in her room or his.

"I want to hear more about you," Graham said, "family, friends, exes."

She laughed and took a sip from her glass. "Plenty of exes." She angled her head demurely. "Well, I'm the only child of a single mother. Sounds like a Lifetime Movie, huh? My father left when I was about five." Her gaze drifted off for a moment. "I never understood why." She frowned. "As a kid I internalized it. It had to be my fault. Right?" She looked at him and then looked away. She shrugged. "I got over it more or less."

"Did you ever see your father after that?"

She shook her head. "Nope. But my mother did everything she could to make up for it. She worked like an indentured servant. Long hours, six and seven days a week." She sipped her drink. "She made sure I never wanted for anything, but that I understood hard work and the importance of education." She rested her forearms on the table. "I think I pretty much spent my life making sure that I lived up to her expectations. Don't get me wrong," she added, holding up her hand. "I don't regret it. It made me the woman that I am."

"Does your mother live in Atlanta?"

Her expression changed. "She passed," she said softly.

Instinctively, he reached across the table and covered her hand with his. The contact was electrifying. His fingers wrapped around her hand.

She exhaled. "It was one of the reasons why I decided to take the job. I would have never come if she... had still been with us."

The waitress returned with their salads. "Your meals will be out shortly. Can I refill your drinks?"

"Yes," Alexis said.

"And you, sir?"

"No. I'm fine. Thanks."

The waitress left.

"What about you? What about your family? Where did your passion for education reform come from?"

"For Barbados or Bajan families, education is paramount. My mum sent me to England when I was ten to live with relatives." He waved his hand. "Let's just say they were strict. My escape then was books." He couldn't tell her his real-life story, how he grew up in spite of what was done to him and how he lived. He didn't want her sympathy. He could have easily been a character in a Charles Dickens novel.

"What about your exes?" she asked, turning him away from his dark thoughts.

"A long list I'm ashamed to say." He pressed his hand to his chest. "It was me not them," he said, feigning sincerity.

Alexis tossed her head back and laughed that throaty,

sexy sound and Graham imagined himself planting kisses along her slender neck, in the hollow of her collarbone…behind her ear.

She settled her attention back on him. "You were telling me on our way down here on the train that you usually try to catch a few shows when you're in town. Music?"

He nodded. "Absolutely. D.C. has some of the best blues and jazz clubs outside of New Orleans and New York."

"I had no idea."

"Then I feel compelled to introduce you to the jazz scene of the nation's capital."

"I'll hold you to that."

He raised his glass in promise.

Their dinner arrived and in between bites they debated about the NBA finals, dished on the demise of the Lakers, offered their own solutions to the communities destroyed by hurricanes and tornadoes, their favorite college players and their draft chances.

Basketball somehow segued to sharing stories about vacations. Alexis told him over bubbles of laughter the trip that she was supposed to take with her best friend Naomi Clarke and never went, but it was where Naomi met her husband. She opened her purse and took out her cell phone and showed him her array of pictures of Naomi and her brand-new goddaughter.

"A real beauty," Graham said of the baby. "How long have you and Naomi been friends?"

"Forever." She giggled. "Not quite. Since college. Same sorority. Roommates. Worked at the same university. And we are like night and day. Let's just say that Naomi is my conscience."

"Really?" His brow rose.

"Hard to believe that anyone would have any influence over me, huh?"

"Yes, very."

She playfully swatted his hand. "What about you—your friend that you went to the game with. He must be a very good friend."

"He is." He told her the story of how they'd met.

"You. Are. Kidding. Me. That's what I call a die-hard fan." She shook her head in bemused disbelief. "To get on a plane to see a game."

Graham shrugged. "In our defense the trip was during the NBA Finals."

"Whatever," she chuckled.

The waitress returned and took away their plates. "Dessert?"

Alexis shook her head.

"I'll take the check," Graham said.

Alexis fingered her purse. *The evening would come to an end in a matter of minutes. Then what?*

"It's still nice out. How about a stroll around the block to walk off this food," he suggested as if he'd read her mind.

After paying the bill, Graham and Alexis stepped out into the moonlit evening. They strolled along E Street for several blocks, quietly taking in the sights, the night-lights that twinkled against the veil of darkness and the illumination of the Washington Monument in the far distance.

"Anything you think we need to add for tomorrow's meeting?" Alexis asked, quietly, not really caring about the answer but only wanting to hear Graham's voice.

"You know what I think?"

She angled her head to look up at him. The deep, dark centers of his eyes picked up the light and reflected it back at her. "No…" she said on a breath. "What *do* you think?"

Graham stopped walking. He clasped her arm and turned her to face him. She glanced up at him, expectant and knowing.

"I think," he stroked the curve of her jaw with the tip of his finger. A shiver rippled through her. "I think that we make a formidable couple."

Couple? But before she could process the implication, he'd lifted her chin and the world around her was blocked out as he lowered his head and touched his lips to hers.

Testing…teasing…tasting…taking.

He cupped the back of her head and eased her into the kiss, deeper and sweeter.

Heat coursed through her even as she shivered against him. He pulled her closer.

Here she was standing in the middle of Washington, D.C., making out with the sexiest man on a public street, and the man was her boss, and people were probably watching, and she hadn't "made out" in public since her high school prom, and she didn't care. She didn't care where she was or what anyone thought. The only thing she cared about was how he was making her feel and she didn't want it to stop.

Graham's hands slid down the sides of her face. Slowly he eased back and looked down into her eyes. "I've wanted to do that from the moment you stepped those long legs into the car at the airport," he breathed against her mouth.

Her heart was pounding like mad her chest. "Funny, I thought the same thing."

He chuckled and ran his finger along her bottom lip, eliciting a sigh from her. "I told you we make a formidable couple." He briefly glanced right then left. "Let's not cause an international incident."

"At least not right here," she said with a wicked gleam in her eyes.

He took her hand and they retraced their steps back to the hotel.

The return trip took an eternity or so it seemed, and they kept stealing surreptitious looks at each other as if to reaffirm to themselves that what they were about to do was real—a game changer.

Electricity snapped between them as they stood pressed side by side in the elevator, working hard to contain themselves in front of the other passengers. The elevator dinged. The doors slid open.

Graham gently gave Alexis's hand a reassuring squeeze. She still had time to back out. What they were about to do was potentially messy and went against every grain of good sense that she had. She ran down the list of why they shouldn't do this even as she slid the card through the slot on the door, pushed it open and stepped inside.

Then she turned into his arms and the heat of his mouth covered hers and she drank in the taste of him as her tongue dueled and danced with his. She still had time to say no, even as his fingers played with the button of her pants, loosened it and they floated silently to the floor. She could bring this all to a halt if she stepped back instead of pressing herself against his rock-hard erection; or if the scent of him didn't arouse her in ways that took her breath away or if his fingers hadn't found their way beneath the elastic band of her panties and eased them down over her hips.

Yes, even then she could have stopped him when his thumb brushed across her pulsing bud and made her inner thighs tremble and her knees weak and a moan escape. She could have stopped him, but hell, she didn't want to.

"It seems you have the advantage," she said in a ragged whisper while Graham rained hot kisses along her exposed neck. "You have me out of mine but I have yet to have you out of yours."

"Don't let anything I'm doing stop you," he whispered as he eased a finger inside of her.

Alexis gasped. Her body arched. She gripped his shoulders and her fingers surely left their imprint as the sensations rolled through her. Pure instinct guided her fingers to pull his jacket from his shoulders, unfasten the tiny white buttons, unbuckle the leather belt, unzip the metal zipper and release him.

Graham gritted his teeth when the butter softness of Alexis's hand encircled and then stroked him ever so gently. The pad of her thumb ran a teasing caress across the head and he nearly lost it. He gripped her wrist. Alexis smiled. She took him by the hand and led him to her bedroom.

Alexis backed into her bedroom with a smoldering look in her eyes that directed Graham to follow her lead. She stopped when she reached the foot of the bed. She stood in front of him, illuminated only by the full moon and starlight that filtered in through the floor-to-ceiling window.

She lifted her blouse over her head, dropped it dramatically to the floor then reached behind her and unhooked her bra, before slowly lowering one strap and then the other. She paused, stripper-style, before she shimmied out of her bra, spun it on her finger much to Graham's delight, and then let it drop. She crooked her finger beckoning him and he walked toward her.

She hooked her thumbs around his loosened pants and pushed them down over his hips. He stepped out of them. Alexis's eyes roved hungrily over him. Graham removed his shirt, tossed it next to his pants. He came toward her. Her breath caught. The determination in his gaze and in his stride was as thrilling as it was frightening.

He hooked his arm around her waist and pulled her nakedness hard and flush against him. He nibbled her bottom lip. "Feel free to stop me," he said, his voice hot. He lifted her up, cupping her derriere in his large hands. She expelled a short gasp and wrapped her legs around his waist. His erection pressed against the slickness of her opening. He bent his knees slightly, shifted Alexis into position and pushed up inside of her.

All of the air rushed from her lungs expelling a cry of indescribable delight. She locked her fingers around his neck and arched her back when he lowered his head to suckle her breasts. The nerves and muscles quivered as if electrified, setting off one jolt after another each time he moved in and out of her, levering her body up and down his erection at will, as if she weighed no more than a loaf of bread.

Incredibly, he managed to walk them to the bed without missing a stroke. He lowered her to the bed and settled between her tight thighs.

His mouth covered hers while his hands caressed her curves, tingled her skin, set her on fire. Now he could have all of her. He looped her legs over the curve of his arms and pushed her thighs back until her ankles rested on his shoulders and then he entered her—fully and completely.

Alexis's eyes flew open. A strangled cry hung in her throat. The overwhelming sensation of him filling her stunned her, stilled her body. The way he had her positioned left her totally open and vulnerable to his every thrust. She could do nothing but take him, stroke after deep stroke. Tears of ecstasy filled her eyes. He rotated his hips so that with each downward thrust he brushed her clit sending jolts of blinding pleasure rushing through her limbs. Ensnared in the throes of sublime joy, she lost all sense of the world around her and became a vessel of pure feeling.

Graham never knew sex could feel this good. From the moment he'd met Alexis he'd tried to imagine what she would feel like draped around him like Christmas wrapping paper. Nothing in his experience had prepared him for the complete surrender of his soul. He could feel her in every inch of his being. He wanted to be everywhere within her at once. He wanted to memorize every curve to take the image with him wherever he went. He wanted to feel this feeling always but the intensity was too great. His heart raced like a stallion let loose on the open pasture. His skin was on fire and he felt the telltale swelling, the tightness in the pit of his belly and she did too.

She stroked his back, cupped his rear end and pulled him closer, harder. Graham groaned and her name hissed through his lips like water tossed on a heated stove.

The rhythm escalated. The panting rose. Sweat popped off their skin. Alexis's fingertips dug into his flesh, holding on because surely she was falling off the face of the earth. Graham touched her center.

Their bodies rose and fell in unison. Pulses quickened. Moans filled the air. Faster. Harder. Now.

Graham ground into her one last time and the explosion burst from him. Her insides gripped him, released him, sucked him and shook her like a rag doll with their intensity.

Wave after wave of pleasure flowed through and between them until they collapsed—beyond spent. Their breathing rapid and sporadic filled the sex-infused air.

Chapter 9

The weight of his body felt good on hers, Alexis thought through the haze of afterglow. *O.M.G.* That was the only coherent thought that she could put together and it kept repeating in her head like a scratched record.

True, she had a fair share of lovers in her life and she was pretty sure that Ian would forever remain in the annals of greatness, but Graham...well...O.M.G. She exhaled a long, satisfying sigh.

"Hmm." He nuzzled her neck and gingerly lifted himself, sliding his weight partially off and only keeping her pinned with his leg draped across her.

Alexis angled her head so that she could look at him. He was even better looking after sex if that was possible. He opened one eye and grinned at her.

"Your skills clearly extend beyond the boardroom," he said, his tone teasing, his British accent heavy. He ran his hand along her hip.

"And you seem to have a full plate of skills yourself," she said over bubbling laughter.

He leaned in and kissed her lightly on the lips. His expression grew serious. "I have a whole platter of skills I want to show you. That was only the appetizer."

Her eyes darkened with desire. She ran her thumb across his lips. "Let me be the first to say bring on the main course, and I will provide the dessert."

She turned him onto his back and straddled him. "How 'bout I get us started," she whispered, before covering his mouth with hers.

Alexis slowly unwound and stretched like a cat. Her foot brushed against the hard lines of Graham's body. She smiled in the semidarkness. He murmured softly in his sleep and reflexively reached out and pulled her back next to him.

Alexis stared up at the ceiling and then turned to peer at the digital clock. It was nearly midnight. She was suddenly ravenous and wondered if she could still order room service. Gingerly she lifted Graham's arm from across her waist and stealthily eased out of the bed and tiptoed to the front room. From the desk she took the faux leather booklet that outlined the hotel services, flipped to "Room Service" and released a sigh of relief to see that they made deliveries until 1:00 a.m. She scrolled through the menu. The way she was feeling everything looked good. She had a good mind to order steak and fries but knew that was ridiculous. Instead she ordered chicken quesadillas, two bowls of black bean soup and two iced teas.

She peeked over her shoulder. Graham was still asleep. She went into the bathroom to freshen up and caught a glimpse of herself in the mirror. She looked like she'd been totally and thoroughly sexed.

Her copper-colored skin was flushed. Her eyes had a new sparkle in them. Her lips were puffy and her spiral twists were all over her head, and although it wasn't apparent to the naked eye her insides still vibrated. She turned on the faucets, rinsed her face and did a quick but thorough wash-up.

"I thought I'd been walked out on until I remembered that this was your room."

A smile pulled across her mouth. She turned to face him as he stood naked and gorgeous in the doorway. "That would have been a little awkward." Her gaze moved up and down his chiseled frame. "I ordered room service. I was suddenly starved."

"A woman who orders room service after making love is a woman after my own heart," he said, pressing his hand to his chest.

She snorted a laugh and tossed him one of the terry robes from the hook near the shower. "At least try to look presentable." She sauntered past him and he gave her behind a playful swat.

Room service arrived and they ate like two people who hadn't eaten a meal in days instead of hours. They chewed and sipped and laughed and talked with their mouths full until every morsel and every drop was gone.

Alexis flopped back onto the bed spread eagle. She was in total heaven. Both of her hungers had been satiated—her hunger for Graham and her appetite.

Graham rolled onto his side to face her. "I'll see you in the morning."

Her eyes fluttered open. Her heart beat just a little faster. "Oh, sure." She made herself smile to push away the funny feeling she suddenly had in the pit of her stomach.

He pressed his lips to her forehead like she'd become a relative instead of a woman he'd done all manner of things to parts of her body that she didn't believe was possible.

Graham pushed up from the bed and went in search of his clothes, putting them on without looking at her, without saying a word.

Alexis's throat tightened. She blinked rapidly to ward off the sting in her eyes.

"Get some rest," he said in parting as he walked out of the bedroom and closed the door softly behind him.

Alexis didn't move. She listened to the sound of her heart beating in the empty room.

Graham had been up with the sun. He'd done the gym, jogged, showered, dressed and found his way down to the lobby. He'd tried everything to shake loose the invisible hold that Alexis had woven around him. The aftereffect of what happened between them last night had shaken him. Making love to a woman was always pleasurable, some more than others. But with Alexis... He sipped his coffee.

Certainly the dynamics of their relationship was permanently altered. But they were adults, consenting adults. He would expect that she would be able to maintain a professional relationship in the workplace. The truth of the matter was that he should not have crossed that invisible line no matter what his body was telling him. It opened the possibilities to all types of repercussions, the least of which could be a lawsuit. He shook his head. She wouldn't do something like that. Would she?

At that moment, Alexis walked into the hotel lobby. Graham spotted her. Flashes of her writhing beneath him, riding him, calling his name played in his head and clouded his thoughts. He felt a stirring in his groin. The question then became, would he be able to remain professional?

Alexis saw him on the far side of the lobby seated near the window. She lifted her chin, steadied her expression and strode toward him. "Good morning." She put her purse down on the small circular table.

"Morning." His gaze took her in. He inhaled her sensual scent. What he wanted to do was take her back upstairs and say the hell with the meeting. That was the problem, he could easily be distracted and lose sight of his objectives because of his attraction to her.

Alexis sat down opposite him and vaguely checked her watch. "Do I have time for a cup?" Her gaze settled in on a space just beyond his shoulder.

"Sure. Light and sweet?"

"Yes."

He got up and went over to the complimentary breakfast bar and prepared a cup of coffee for Alexis.

Alexis couldn't remember the last time she'd been this nervous and on edge with a man. The morning after was always a little dicey but the fact that he was her boss added a new level of trickery.

Graham set the cup of coffee down in front of her and took his seat.

"Thanks."

He wrapped his hands around his cup. "I wanted to stay last night."

"You don't have to explain."

"I know, but I want to anyway." He swallowed. "I left because I didn't want anyone to see me coming from your room this morning."

She blinked back her surprise. "Oh," she managed.

"There are quite a few people in town for the education summit. Many of whom know me. I won't risk your reputation or that of R.E.A.L. by possibly being seen by a colleague coming from your room at sunrise."

For the first time since he'd walked out of her hotel room the knot in the center of her stomach began to unravel. She visibly relaxed.

"I am honored that you were willing to defend my honor, kind sir," she said in her best Scarlett O'Hara voice.

Graham laughed from deep in his belly. Alexis's warm smile matched his. The band of tension snapped.

Graham and Alexis were the third group on the list to make their presentation. Working in tandem, they put on a show that dazzled the committee with their ideas, methods of implementation and long-term outcomes. They worked together like a perfect melody, playing off of each other, supporting the notes, knowing when to reach high and dip low. They harmonized and when it was appropriate they showcased their solo skills.

When they walked out they knew they'd made a major impression with the committee, but it was the energy that flowed between them and electrified them that was undeniable.

They both felt it as they packed up and walked out of the conference hall, when they stole looks at each other or casually brushed each other's hand. It was like rubbing two sticks together: sparks start, sputter, catch, smoke and finally…fire.

The flames engulfed them both as they made love from the front door of Graham's hotel room to the back. They tried positions that defied physics and they laughed and kissed and teased and touched until they collapsed in a tangle of damp sheets and limp limbs.

While Alexis rested in the bedroom, Graham went into the living area and made some phone calls and reservations for later that night.

His conversation with Tracy was productive, but a bit strained. She sounded distant during the call and when he asked her if something was bothering her she insisted that everything was fine; she was "very busy." He let it go, but he planned to address it when he was back in New York. He'd sent a text to Blake with the time and address for the club. A few days earlier Blake had advised he would be in D.C. for business. Alexis peeked out from beneath the sheet when Graham walked back into the room.

"Missed you," she said in a husky whisper.

Graham chuckled. "No, you didn't. You were knocked out."

She huffed. "I still missed you…in my sleep."

"I'm honored." He plopped down on the side of the bed, intentionally giving it an extra bounce. "Hope you're up for going out tonight. I made reservations at Smoke."

"Sure." She rose up on her elbow. "Smoke?"

"Jazz and blues club in Georgetown. And if you're a good girl I may introduce you to the headliners." He pressed his finger on the tip of her nose.

"Really? Who's performing?"

"Quinten Parker and Rafe Lawson."

She sat straight up in bed. "Get out!" She slapped his thigh. "You know them?"

He grinned. "Yes."

She brought her knees up to her chest and draped her arms across them. She looked him straight in the eye. Her right brow rose. "Now I'm impressed."

He chuckled and shook his head. "All this time I thought you were impressed with my dashing good looks, intelligence, wit and prowess in bed, when it's really who I know. I'm crushed."

Alexis rolled her eyes. "Right," she droned. "Anyway, is this a dress-up place or casual...?"

"Casual." His gaze trailed over her face. He pulled the sheet away from her. "Although on a personal note I much prefer this look on you." He leaned in and kissed her long and sweet and slow before covering her body with his.

Chapter 10

By the time Graham and Alexis arrived at Smoke the club was already crowded and the evening was in full swing. The dimly lit atmosphere, the lush leather booths and round tables draped in burgundy linen gave the illusion that the expansive space actually lived up to its name. There was a four-piece band on stage playing some original music. A hostess showed Graham and Alexis to their table that had a perfect view of the stage.

Graham helped Alexis into her seat. She took a look around. "This reminds me of a lounge in Atlanta, Café 290. My friend Naomi and I used to go a couple of times a month...until she got married." She smiled wistfully.

"If you like the lounge scene, good music, adult crowds, there are plenty of places I can show you in New York."

Her heart jumped. She hadn't wanted to think beyond

this weekend, this time of make-believe away from the real world. When they returned to New York they'd be back to employer-employee. At some point they were going to have to discuss this thing between them.

Graham suddenly stood and waved his hand. Alexis looked over her shoulder and watched a damned good-looking man with a sexy stroll come toward them. She barely noticed the woman he was with.

Graham and his friend did the man hug and the black-man-handshake thing before turning to the ladies.

"Alexis, this is Blake Stevens. Blake, Alexis Montgomery."

Blake extended his hand to Alexis. "Pleasure. I've heard great things about you. This is my colleague, Sydni Lawson. We're working on a business venture."

"Nice to meet you," Sydni said. Blake pulled out a chair for her next to Alexis.

"Lawson?" Alexis said, "Related to Rafe Lawson?"

Sydni grinned and a soft dimple dented her right cheek.

"Cousin. My dad is Rafe's great-uncle."

"So *your* uncle is Senator Branford Lawson."

Sydni nodded. "Uncle Branford's name stretches far and wide," she said in jest. "I don't get to see the family as often as I would like so when Blake told me he was meeting Graham to listen to Rafe's set, I had to come. Plan to surprise him."

Alexis lowered her voice. "When Graham said that Quinten Parker and Rafe Lawson were going to be here I would have found a way to get here with or without him."

Sydni laughed. "I know what you mean. I've been following Quinten's career for years. Then I find out that my cousin is just as bad as Quinten and building a following, which by the way is probably turning my uncle's hair seriously gray." She giggled.

"I can imagine," Alexis said.

A waiter approached. "What can I get you all?"

The group placed their drink and dinner orders, just as the lights dimmed even further and the soft spotlight hit the stage.

"Blake said that you two were colleagues. What business are you in?" Alexis asked.

"I'm the VP of Epic International, my area of expertise is international marketing and publicity with a specialization in global branding. It's a mouthful, but basically my job is to establish an individual, group, business or idea in the global arena."

Alexis nodded, intrigued with the concept. "We'll have to talk. Maybe we can work together."

"Sure. I'd love to. I'm based in Louisiana, but I come to New York often. I have several clients there. Next time I'm in town I'll definitely call you."

"Great."

Smoke's MC stepped into the light, greeted all the guests and introduced the Parker Lawson Trio.

Quinten, smooth and easy with his New York swagger, came onto the stage and sat down behind the piano, his trademark locks falling down to the middle of his back, held together at the base of his neck with a black band.

Next came Rafe Lawson, the essence of Southern charm, the sensuality that exuded from his every movement was mesmerizing. He carried his sax across his chest and close to his heart. He adjusted the ninety-degree-angled microphone.

And then Rae Parker walked to the center spotlight.

She gave each of the men a short nod and a smile. Rae had begun to make a name for herself as a singer and spoken-word artist when she'd met Quinten—at least that's what the tabloids and entertainment shows said and it had never been disputed. They'd been married for almost a decade.

"Good evening, ladies and gentlemen," Rae said, her voice silky and inviting. "These very handsome men will back me up as we do our own brand of jazz, with some familiar songs mixed in." She twisted the mic in the stand. "So please, enjoy." She gave a quick glance over her shoulder and Quinten's fingers glided across the keys and were joined by Rafe's soothing sax. After a few chords, Rae's sultry voice blended in seamlessly with the music crooning a Betty Carter tune.

The trio played for more than an hour with every number getting better and better. Each member took their moment to shine. It was over all too soon. The trio took their bows and then did two more numbers before leaving the stage to rousing applause.

"That was worth every minute," Alexis said.

"I knew Q's work, but my cousin really has some skills," Sydni added.

"Let's head backstage for a few while they get ready for their next set," Graham said, taking out his credit card to pay for dinner.

They got up and followed Graham around the tables, then waited while he spoke to the security guard at the entrance that led to the hallway and the dressing rooms.

The guard opened the door and the quartet walked down the hallway until they came to the partially opened door of one of the dressing rooms. Deep laughter rolled out into the hallway.

Graham tapped on the frame of the door and stuck his head in. "I heard some players were in the house," he said over his chuckles.

"G!" Quinten greeted. He hopped down from the side of the table. "You made it. Come on in, man."

Graham walked in with Blake, Alexis and Sydni on his heels.

"Blake. What's up, man?" Rafe said, clapping him on the back then doing the same to Graham. His eyes widened and his smile froze in place when he spotted his cousin. "Sydni?"

She grinned and walked over to be enveloped in a tight hug. She kissed his cheek. "Still handsome, I see. Keeping the women at bay?" Her eyes sparkled.

"Oh, *cher,* you wound me." He winked at her and slid his arm around her waist.

"Quinten, Rafe, this is Alexis Montgomery. Alexis, Quinten Parker, Rafe Lawson."

Alexis had died and gone to testosterone heaven. The room oozed manliness, with one handsome hunk outdoing the next.

"It is so incredible to meet both of you." Her face beamed.

"Pleasure is mine." Rafe took her hand and brought it to his lips. He placed a feather-soft kiss on her knuckles.

"Watch him," Quinten said with a twinkle in his eyes. He took her hand from Rafe's. "Nice to meet you." He turned to Sydni. "You're related to this guy?"

"We all have our crosses to bear." She grinned at her cousin, just as Rae walked in.

"This is where the real party is I see." She sauntered over to her husband who made the introductions.

"Fabulous performance," Alexis said to her.

"Thank you. Working with them makes it easy. Speaking of which, we need to get ready for the next set."

Goodbyes were said, promises made to stay in touch and Alexis and Sydni exchanged phone numbers when they'd gotten outside.

"What a night," Alexis said, settling into the cab, the sound of pleasure underscoring her voice. "Thank you so much."

"They were even better than I thought. I haven't heard Rae in a while. The trio thing is a bit new."

"It works."

Graham draped his arm across the back of the seat and let his fingers drift onto her shoulder.

She leaned her head back and closed her eyes. This time tomorrow they would be back in New York. The thought made her stomach tighten.

"We need to talk," he said as if once again reading her mind.

She opened her eyes and angled her head to look at him. He was staring at her.

"I know."

He kissed her forehead and then drew her close. "We'll have to find a way to make it work."

"Discreetly. I don't want anyone thinking…"

"I know and they won't."

"At work it must be strictly business."

"Absolutely. But the nights belong to us."

A slow smile moved across her mouth. She looked into his eyes. "I think I like the sound of that."

"So do I."

* * *

They spent the night together in Alexis's hotel room. When they returned from the club there was no real discussion. They seemed to instinctively understand that they were going to be together. It was all so easy as if they'd been lovers for years instead of two days and understood each other in ways that took most couples years to achieve.

"I had an incredible time tonight. Wait until I tell Naomi. She's going to be so jealous." She chuckled lightly as she stepped out of her shoes and put them in the closet.

"How about some wine?"

"Sounds good. I'm going to take a quick shower."

"Hmm, how about if I bring the bottle and join you."

"That sounds even better. As a matter of fact…" She walked up to him and tugged on the lapel of his jacket. "Why don't I run us a bath and we can sit *and* sip."

"That sounds even better." He kissed her lightly on the lips. "You run the water. I'm going across the hall for a minute."

"Sure. Take the key card," she called out while she walked into the bathroom.

Alexis turned on the faucets in the deep soaker tub and added some of the bath salts that the hotel provided. Within moments the room filled with aromatic steam. She quickly arranged the towels within easy reach and hung two terry robes on the hooks behind the door and then pressed the button on the panel that piped in music. She checked the water and turned it off. She began to undress, anticipation building in her veins. She dropped her blouse to the floor.

"That's the kind of show I could watch every night," Graham said from his bird's-eye position at the door.

Alexis glanced seductively over her shoulder and gave him a come-hither smile. "You could make the progress much quicker," she said, her voice heated by the light of desire in his eyes.

"The lady is always right." He came up behind her and unfastened her bra.

His nimble fingers slid the straps off her shoulders then moved around and cupped her breasts possessively in his palms. He teased her nipples until her sighs deepened to moans. He placed hot kisses down her neck and along the ridge of her spine. She trembled each time his mouth connected with her flesh. His fingers trailed down her curves, across her stomach that fluttered against his touch.

"I want you," he breathed hotly into her ear. He unfastened her slacks, pushed them and her panties down and over her hips. She quickly stepped out of them.

Graham's arm snaked tightly around her waist, binding her to him. His erection pressed rock hard against her lower back. His hand moved down between her legs. She drew in a sharp breath and he groaned in satisfaction to find her wet and ready.

He unbuttoned his pants with his free hand and let them fall. "The bath can wait," he said on a ragged breath, "but I can't." He bent her forward, positioned himself between her legs and entered her in one, long deep stroke with such force that she had to grip the edge of the sink to keep from being lifted off of her feet.

Graham alternated between caressing her breasts and stroking her swollen clit, sending jolt after jolt of pleasure through her veins.

A myriad of sensations swirled within her, so intense at times that she could not hold back her cries of joy and then she looked up and saw their images in the mirror, more like apparitions in the steamy room, and it pushed her even further to the edge.

"Come with me," he demanded, nearly pulling completely out of her, only leaving enough of himself inside to tease her opening.

She whimpered. Her insides instinctively contracted. She gripped the edge tighter. The backs of her legs tightened. Her inner thighs trembled. Heat flooded her belly. Her head spun.

Graham pushed slowly back inside her. So slow she thought she would go crazy—and then again, and again. Tears pushed out from the corner of her eyes. She threw her head back in a fit of agony and ecstasy. Graham rotated his pelvis and Alexis matched him move for move until all that could be heard in the heated room was the sound of their panting breaths and the slap of skin against skin.

Graham grabbed her hips, controlling her ability to move and he took her mercilessly, the urge for release boiling like a volcano inside of her as he banged against her.

Somehow she managed to snake her hand between her legs and found his full sac. Gently she squeezed, once, twice and an animal-like growl rose up from his throat as his erection stiffened even more, filled to bursting and exploded into her sending shock waves of jism roaring through her body as she shuddered and jolted in a release that eclipsed explanation. If Graham wasn't holding on to her for dear life she would have collapsed on the floor.

Every nerve ending sizzled. Her legs felt like spaghetti and her girl wouldn't stop purring.

With difficulty and great reluctance Graham eased out of her and slowly turned her around. He tucked his finger beneath her chin and tilted her head up to his. He lowered his mouth to hers for a long, deep kiss.

When he leaned back his eyes were at half-mast. Pure satisfaction defined his face. "Woman…" That was all he could say.

"A man of many words," she teased in a lazy voice.

"How about that bath. I could use a good soak." He took her hand and they walked to the tub. He checked the water, turned on the faucet to add more hot water. He got in first. Alexis got in and sat between his legs so that she could lean back against him.

When she lowered herself into the water her entire body sighed with pleasure. The water, just shy of very hot, massaged and loosened her overworked muscles that had been tested beyond endurance.

She rested her head on his chest and her hands on his thighs. She let her eyes drift closed as the steam wafted up around her.

Graham reached for the soap from the dish and lathered the white cloth before gently washing her neck, down the valley of her breasts and across her stomach.

"Open your legs," he whispered in her ear while he replaced the cloth with the bar of soap and tenderly caressed her swollen breasts until they were sudsy and smooth. He continued administering to her breasts, re-igniting the flames of arousal.

Alexis moaned softly when his finger slid between her slick folds and teased and stroked while her fingertips pressed deeper and deeper into his thighs. She bit down on her bottom lip to keep from crying out when he pushed two fingers inside of her.

Graham was fully erect now and the overwhelming need to bury himself inside of her again was more than he could fight back. As if she weighed no more than a bag of groceries he managed to raise her up just enough for him to position himself.

She knew what he wanted and she wanted it, too, so she maneuvered her body until she had him between her legs, beneath her opening and then lowered herself down onto him and it stole her breath.

For several seconds neither of them could move, overtaken by the intensity of their union.

Graham held his breath, gritted his teeth and lowered his head to rest on the back of hers while he silently prayed to regain some sense of control.

"Bend your knees and lean back against me."

Alexis followed his instructions and he adjusted his position accordingly before turning on the jets of the Jacuzzi.

"Spread your legs wider," he ordered in a raspy whisper.

She did and the pulse of the spray beat against her opening and sent shocks jolting through her. She gasped. Her hips instinctively rose toward the source of the pleasure then lowered. They both groaned with pleasure.

The pulse of the water combined with Graham's incredibly hard erection that filled every inch of her and pressed against that spot had her dizzy and trembling. She wanted it all at once but the pleasure was so intense she felt as if she was going to pass out and the sensations kept climbing higher.

Graham suddenly pushed upward, the jets pulsed and

Alexis exploded into a millions pieces of herself, spewing all over as the climax ripped through her and Graham stroked and teased every iota of it out of her.

"You're pretty hot for a cool Brit," she said lazily, her body still humming.

Graham stroked her hair away from her face and kissed the back of her neck. "Don't let the accent fool you."

And like the previous night, Graham was gone before sunrise. This time that funny feeling in her stomach was absent when she rolled over and found the spot next to her still warm but empty. They met in the lobby and caught an early train Sunday morning. By that afternoon they would be back to the real world.

Chapter 11

The train ride back went from easy and comfortable to surreal before they hit Maryland. Their days together seemed like a dream that she was slowly awakening from. The closer the train drew to their final destination the more reality sank in. Even though they'd come to an understanding it was still going to take some adjustment to come down from this amazing high.

She turned to glance at Graham. He was dozing next to her. She studied him in repose, and everything that he'd said to her, the way he moved, smiled, laughed and made love to her rolled through her thoughts and that thing that kept her anchored and focused broke loose and she felt herself being taken away on a raging tide of emotions. The first problem was sleeping with her boss. The second problem was having feelings for him.

How could that be? They barely had time to get to

know each other. But it didn't seem to matter. Time wasn't a factor. They did know each other. They were inside each other's heads from the very beginning. And now he was in her soul. That was the dangerous part, the part that had her fearful of the days ahead. She couldn't get caught up in feelings and lose her edge or her perspective.

Alexis turned away and drew in a breath of resolve. *It was only great sex with a sexy man.* That was all. From here on out it was business as usual.

The cab ride from Penn Station to Sutton Place was awkward for lack of a better word. It was almost as if a third party, a stranger was sitting between them and they didn't want the stranger to overhear their conversation—so they didn't talk, at least not about anything of substance.

Mercifully the ride was short and before long they were greeted by Glen at the front of the building and then they were on the elevator.

"O-kay," Alexis said on a breath, dragging out the word as the elevator pinged on her floor. "Talk to you tomorrow."

"Yes, tomorrow, then."

Her gaze flicked toward him but she dared not look too long or else he would see all of the questions and anxiety in her eyes. But what she did catch in his expression momentarily stilled her heart. *Nothing.*

Alexis adjusted her tote on her shoulder and pulled her small luggage behind her. She could barely see to get the key in the lock of her apartment door through the cloud of tears burning her eyes.

Once inside she didn't try to hold back any longer and

the tears ran down her high cheeks. Just the idea that some man had her crying turned her tears into angry ones at herself. It was clear from the expression on his face that it truly was just a romp. How many others were there? Was she the first from the office or had there been others?

What difference did it make? She knew going in that sleeping with the boss was trouble on simmer. Did she really believe that mind-blowing sex equaled a relationship?

She swiped at her eyes with the back of her hand and tossed her tote onto the club chair in her bedroom. *Get it together, girl. Graham Stone is just a man, not the Holy Grail. He thinks he's mastered that British cool. He hasn't seen Atlanta chilly.*

Her first bout of anxiety was allayed when she didn't run into Graham on her way out of the apartment building en route to the office. Throughout the night she'd had recurring dreams of her and Graham in an elevator. In one version they were trapped for hours and had nothing to say to each other. In another dream he came on the elevator with another woman who was glued to him at the hip. In the third version he got on the elevator and he didn't see her or at least he acted like he didn't. The different versions continued all night in a loop. She awoke cranky and edgy and tried to burn off some of her unevenness by working out with her favorite exercise DVD. It helped a little. At least she didn't feel like kicking a cat or rolling her eyes at an old lady.

When she arrived at the office it was still early and only the IT division had anyone in the office. Her goal was to ground herself back in her work. Reclaim her sense of balance through what she did best so that when she did see Graham again she would have resurrected the wall of work. He would stay on his side and she would stay on hers. When they needed to they would meet in the middle, but never again would she cross that line.

By eight she began to hear the buzz of the office coming to life. In the hour and a half that she'd been at her desk she'd thoroughly reviewed all of the notes and reports from the meetings in D.C., answered email, consolidated the notes and prepared a final report for distribution at the department meeting, and added new names to her contact list. With each task she gained a little bit more of her sense of self and pushed thoughts and feelings about Graham into the background.

Alexis glanced up at the sound of the light knocking on the frame of her partially opened door. "Claire. Hi. Good morning. Come on in."

Claire stepped inside, looking stylish as always in a beautiful lavendar-colored two-piece skirt suit. "Welcome back. How was the trip?"

Clearly she had no idea that was a loaded question. "Thanks. I was only out of the office for a day, but it feels longer. The trip was very productive. I feel strongly about our position and that the decision of the committee will be favorable."

"Excellent."

"What did I miss?"

"Nothing that I couldn't handle. The usual office stuff. A few phone calls from some of our subcontractors, nothing major."

"Which subcontractors?"

"We recently signed a contract with Horizon. They provide a lot of the software that we use in the classrooms and the teaching aids. They wanted to come in to discuss some new products."

Alexis nodded as she listened.

"And Happy Faces our uniform supplier has some discounts on their boys and girls slacks that they wanted us to know about."

"I didn't realize that we had our own uniform supplier," Alexis said, clearly surprised.

"Yes, Mr. Stone wants R.E.A.L. to be self-contained. He wants us to be able to fulfill every aspect of our children's educational experience. We get bids from the best and the least expensive to pass on to our parents."

Alexis hummed in appreciation. She couldn't help but admire Graham and all of the work he'd put into building this organization. It was really quite amazing and she was sure that there was much more for her to learn. Finding out everything there was to know about Graham Stone's organization was going to be her mission. There was much more to him and this company than what was put on paper. Knowledge was power and she never reveled in being powerless.

"Have you had breakfast?" Claire asked. "I can order out or get you something from the kitchen."

"Something from the kitchen will be fine. Coffee and do we have any yogurt?"

"Light and sweet?"

"Yes."

"Any particular flavor for the yogurt?"

"No, whatever is around. Well, anything other than strawberry."

Claire grinned. "That's so funny, Mr. Stone doesn't like strawberries either," she said on her way out.

An unexpected jolt hit her at that bit of revelation.

Strawberries made her itch. She wondered what was at the root of Graham's aversion.

"I arranged for us to have a private lunch in the small conference room to review the upcoming project in California," Tracy was saying. She sat on the opposite side of Graham's desk. She crossed her long legs to reveal a good deal of her toned thigh.

Graham stared out the window, listening but not paying attention. His thoughts were elsewhere, and for the first time since he'd been on this quest to build his organization, he wished he was anyplace other than at the office. He wanted to be in bed with Alexis, with her legs wrapped around him and the warm sweetness of her voice breathing his name in his ear.

"Graham!"

Graham's gaze snapped back to attention. He blinked Tracy into focus while he slowly angled his head in her direction. "I'm sorry. What were you saying?"

She jutted her chin. "I was talking about the California project."

He nodded. "Let's talk about it a little later." He tapped his index finger absently against the desk.

Tracy frowned. She settled her features into a calm expression. "Sure." She pushed up from her seat. She held her iPad to her chest. "We can talk later."

"Hmm."

She started for the door and then stopped. "Is everything all right? Is something bothering you?"

He swung his chair to face her. "No. Why?"

She gave a slight shrug. "You don't seem yourself. I've never known you to not want to discuss business. That's all."

He offered up a vague smile. "First time for everything I suppose. We'll get to it in a day or two. Promise."

She tugged in a breath. "Whenever you're ready."

"Thanks. Close the door on your way out, would you?"

She threw him a look of discontent before she practically stomped out of the office.

Graham swung his chair back around so that he faced the window. He was pretty sure Alexis was in her office. He was sure if he gave it some thought he could come up with a plausible explanation for marching into her office, locking the door and having her on the love seat. It would be tight considering that they both had long limbs, but it would be worth it.

He shook his head quickly. Now he was losing it. Fantasizing about making love to Alexis when he should be concentrating on business was becoming more of the norm rather than the exception. He shifted in his seat and stroked his chin. Alexis had gotten to him, unlike any other woman that he'd encountered. But he was her boss and he needed to keep that in the forefront of his head.

If he continued to pursue the relationship it could cause numerous problems, especially if it didn't work out. But dammit, he wanted her, really wanted her and he was going to have to find the self-control to keep their relationship under control and out of the way. It was going to be a balancing act. He was game. He hoped that she was, too. He got up from his desk, took the elevator to her floor and strode down the corridor to her office.

Alexis was sipping on her coffee and reading one of the many articles on R.E.A.L. when she sensed Graham's presence. She looked up and her heart banged in her chest. He was standing in the threshold of her office door.

"Mind if I come in?"

"No. Of course not." She shoved the article back into the folder and closed it.

Graham strolled in with his hands in his pockets and gazed casually around taking in the space as if it was the first time he'd been there.

He stopped in front of her desk. She should have stood up so he wouldn't have the advantage of standing over her. But her legs felt weak.

"What can I do for you?"

He pointed his chin in the direction of the chair next to her desk. "Mind if I sit?"

"Please."

He eased down into the side chair. "How are you?" he asked with such a soft tenderness that it made her heart ache.

She swallowed. "I'm good. You?"

He rocked his jaw for a moment while he worked out what he was going to say. He leaned forward and rested his forearms on his thighs. "I'm thinking that I was a bit of an ass last evening on the lift."

She bit back her surprise.

"I came off as indifferent. It's what I wanted you to think…that I didn't care."

"And…"

He looked into her eyes. "I do care. But I can't let that get in the way of our work here. In the office it has to be totally business. And if you want…more…if you want to see where this can go then we have the nights. I need to know if that's enough for you."

Alexis let herself breathe in relief. Although they'd

tentatively agreed on how to proceed with this relationship, Graham's behavior when they'd returned negated all of that. And now here he was presenting his case. She didn't know what to think or what was real; the man sitting in front of her or the one she'd shared the elevator with.

She linked her fingers together on top of the desk. "Why don't we get through the day and…talk about it over dinner."

His eyes darkened. "My place or yours?"

A slow smile moved across her mouth. "I assume you can cook with all the food you bought."

"I know my way around the kitchen."

"Then I guess it's your place."

"Eight?"

"See you there. Should I bring anything?"

"A toothbrush." He rose from his seat. "See you at the staff meeting."

Chapter 12

The 10:00 a.m. staff meeting was lively and informative. Alexis presented her notes on the meetings with the Secretary of Education and the subcommittee and listened attentively to the feedback, which was wholly positive. Of the team members that were present Tracy was unusually quiet. She didn't even offer a left-handed comment or try to poke holes in Alexis's presentation. Alexis made a mental note of it. She was pretty sure that Tracy's reticence would manifest itself in some other way. How, was the question.

"Thank you, everyone," Graham said, effectively ending the meeting. "We're on track for all current projects and everyone is up to speed on what we have on the table. Have a good week, everyone, and my door, as always, is open. Thanks."

One by one the team began to file out, talking among

themselves in twos and threes. Alexis watched as Tracy and another associate, Shawn Stevenson, walked out with their heads close together.

She didn't know Shawn. She'd only been briefly introduced and in the short period of time that she'd been with R.E.A.L. she hadn't had the opportunity to interact with her. Apparently Shawn and Tracy were close at least at work. She hoped that over time she would also develop some close friendships at R.E.A.L. She missed having a close girlfriend nearby like the relationship she shared with Naomi. She never realized or appreciated just how much their friendship meant to her until Naomi had gotten married and moved away.

Although she had male companionship and had embarked on the relationship with Ian, it wasn't the same. There was a bond between women that was just as integral to their well-being and sense of balance as a good diet. She was missing her sisterhood meal.

"Nice job," Graham said, coming up to her side as she gathered her belongings.

She briefly glanced up. "Thanks."

"I find that I enjoy watching you at whatever you do," he said soft enough for only her ears.

Her pulse jumped. When she stole a glance at him he was checking his cell phone, before walking out as if he hadn't just tossed a lit match on her very combustible insides. She smiled to herself, walked out of the conference room and turned down the corridor toward the staff lounge.

The instant she walked in she sensed the immediate shift in the vibe of the room. Tracy and Shawn were sitting at a round table and Alexis had the distinct impression that she'd been the topic of conversation.

"Hello, ladies," Alexis greeted and then walked to the coffee machine.

"Getting settled in?" Shawn asked.

"Pretty much. It's a lot to take in. R.E.A.L. has a great deal of moving parts."

"Yes, it would be more difficult for an outsider to grasp all of the nuts and bolts," Tracy said, before bringing the cup of coffee to her lips. She kept her gaze lowered.

Alexis gritted her teeth to keep from saying something out of line. She poured her coffee into a paper cup and grabbed some sweetener. "Yes, I have a lot of work to do but I believe that I was hired because I'm up to the challenge." She looked directly at Tracy. "Like all of us," she added to soften the sting. "Have a great day, ladies." She turned and walked out.

She returned to her office. Maybe what she needed to do in addition to understanding the nuances of the company and her boss was get to know what made her staff tick—who they were and how they'd gotten their jobs. However, if the taint of animosity went beyond Tracy, she didn't want to disturb the hornets' nest. Rather than contact HR for the personnel files, she'd do things the old-fashioned way: girl talk over lunch. And if that didn't work, pillow talk was bound to do the trick.

When she returned to her office she checked with Claire to see if she had any lunch plans. She did, so they scheduled lunch for the following day. Alexis felt that she could trust Claire. At least she hoped that her instincts were correct.

The rest of the day sped by filled with reading, phone calls and scheduling site visits to the schools under the

R.E.A.L. umbrella in the coming weeks. Before she knew it the staff was starting to head home for the day.

Claire stuck her head in the door. "I'm going to leave. Do you need anything before I go?"

"No. Thanks. I'm right behind you."

"Okay. Have a good evening."

"You, too." She saved the files she was working on, shut down her computer and gathered up her belongings. *Three hours until dinner with Graham.* She left the building with an extra bounce in her step.

If Graham had wound up in any other profession he would have certainly been a chef. He loved to cook and shop for food—in abundance—a desire born of never having enough to eat, to drink, to wear, to love. His young life, the part that molded him was filled with unmet want, a never-ending hunger that he struggled daily to fill. When he came of age he promised himself that he would never be hungry again, that he would never want for anything again, and he wanted the same for all the other little boys and girls whose lives were relegated to that of deprivation.

He took two steaks out of the refrigerator as soon as he'd arrived at his apartment, checked his wine cabinet for the right bottle, selected a handful of baby potatoes, and the fixings for a mixed green salad. Simple but delicious, especially after he added his special homemade steak sauce. He smiled while he worked anticipating the look of delight on Alexis face when she sank her teeth into the steak.

He put the wine to chill while he seasoned the steak and prepared the potatoes and salad. Once everything was done he had time to take a quick shower, select some music for atmosphere and wait for Alexis's arrival.

At seven-thirty his doorbell chimed. *Early*. He liked that. He set down his glass of wine and went to open the door fully anticipating taking the kiss he'd been thinking about all day.

"Tracy...what are you doing here? How did you get in the building?"

"The doorman was busy. I know I should have called first." She almost looked apologetic. "But I really need to talk to you face-to-face and you've been...distant and distracted. I thought that maybe away from the office we could talk...like we always do. I thought maybe we could walk down to that new café on First..."

"Tracy, this is not cool. You need to leave. We'll talk, tomorrow, at the office." His tone was pleasant but undeniably firm. "Good night."

Her eyes burned but she wouldn't give him the satisfaction of seeing her cry. "I totally understand. I'm just worried about you. That's all. And you're right I shouldn't have come here like this. No worries, it won't happen again."

His stance relaxed a bit. "Thank you." He put his hand on her shoulder. "Tomorrow."

She gave him a tight smile. "Good night." She turned and walked away.

All he could think was that he didn't want Alexis to walk off of that elevator. Although what he did after hours in his home was his business, it would still be incredibly awkward requiring explanations that he wasn't inclined to give. Not to mention the position it would put Alexis in.

He realized that he and Tracy had a complicated relationship. Not that it was anything beyond business, but there were often times, because they worked so closely together, that he got the sense that given the opportunity she would take it further. Showing up on his doorstep only confirmed what he'd been thinking. He was sure that things would have been even more dicey had he hired her for Alexis's job. They would have had to spend even more time together. Hopefully, he'd made himself very clear with her just now and they wouldn't have to address or revisit it again.

He released a sigh of relief and slowly closed the door.

Vacillating between anger and humiliation, Tracy got in her car and as she turned her head ever so slightly to close her door, her heart stopped. Walking into the building and being greeted by the doorman—whom *she'd* had to dodge to get in—was Alexis. Her cheeks heated.

So something *was* going on between them. She wasn't imagining things. She knew she took a risk coming to Graham's apartment like that but men didn't turn down her advances. The reality that Graham did stung her more than she realized and it escalated her distaste for Alexis even more. What was so special about her? Not only did Alexis take the job that she deserved but obviously had the *very personal* attention of Graham, as well. She sat there for several minutes more as if she could erase what she'd seen. Of course she couldn't and the image burned into her brain as she tore away from the curb.

Alexis darted into the building and up to her apartment. She'd made a quick run to the market to pick up a bottle of wine. She was sure that the way Graham shopped he had plenty of wine. But she refused to show up empty-handed or at least more in her hand than her toothbrush. The tickle of expectation made her giggle.

It was crazy how things had gone from zero to sixty in the blink of an eye. This was so unlike her but she didn't want to be any other way.

She checked her reflection in the mirror, slipped her cell phone, toothbrush and keys into the pocket of her jogging jacket and headed out.

Moments later she was ringing Graham's bell.

"Thought you would never get here," Graham teased, pulling her into the apartment and fully up against him to drown in a kiss that would wash away the unsettling memory of Tracy's unannounced appearance.

"Well, good evening to you, too," she said, a bit breathless when he released her. Happiness lit up her eyes. She held out the bottle of wine.

"Thanks." He took the bottle of wine in one hand and slid his other arm around her waist. "But I told you that you only needed your toothbrush."

She tapped the pocket on her jacket and winked at him. They walked together into his living area. The music was on but so low and gentle that it was part of the atmosphere rather than an attention getter.

"Mmm, something smells delicious," Alexis said before slipping out of her jacket and sitting on the couch.

"Ready to eat?"

"Starved."

"Great. We can eat in the living room or here at the island."

"The island is fine with me." She got up from the

couch and crossed the space to the kitchen. "Can I help with anything?"

"No, not this time. Tonight you're my guest. Next time you can cook, clean and even take out the trash if you want to," he said, laughing.

"I think I'll milk the guest thing for as long as possible."

"Not a problem. Wine?"

"Sure."

He took out two wineglasses from the overhead cabinet. He poured them each a glass from the bottle he'd chilled and lifted his glass for a toast.

"To a long and unforgettable night."

Alexis smiled, tapped her glass lightly against his and took a sip. "Hmm, this is good."

"Blake actually recommended it to me a few months back."

"The man knows his wines." She took a good look around his apartment as she'd only gotten a brief glimpse the day she'd moved in. The setup was very similar to hers. She wandered over to the massive bookcases and took a closer look at the volumes that covered the gamut of topics from religion, to politics, biographies, thrillers and there were two shelves dedicated to books in French and Japanese. She plucked a book from the shelf. "You speak French and Japanese?"

"I read better than I speak, but yes. And you do as well. French, *oui?*"

She smiled. "*Oui.* I'm a bit rusty, though."

"We'll have to practice on each other sometime."

Why did every other thing that came out of his mouth always ring with double meaning? "Sure." She returned the book to the shelf and then noticed a medal enclosed in a small glass box. She looked closer. It was from the U.S. Navy for meritorious service.

She turned to him. "You were in the navy?"

"Yes." He forked one of the steaks onto her plate and the other onto his. He barely glanced up.

"Were you…in battle?"

"Yes."

She crossed the room and came to sit at the island counter. Graham was focused on preparing their plates. "When?"

"I joined the navy at seventeen." His eyes took on a hard look. "Right out of high school."

"I didn't know that noncitizens could join the service."

He looked at her. "I was born here but I was sent to Barbados when I was two, then shipped off to England. That's where I spent my growing up. Came back when I was done with school and joined the navy. Did two tours." He turned toward the fridge and took out the bowl of salad and put it on the counter between them. "While I was enlisted I got my BA, then my master's. Traveled the world, learned French and Japanese." The corner of his mouth quirked into a brief smile. "Finally settled down in New York. More wine?" He held up the bottle.

"Sure. Thanks. You make it sound so matter of fact, so ordinary."

"Isn't it?"

"Maybe for some people but not for most."

He shrugged slightly. "I don't really think about it."

"That medal, it's for flying, correct?"

"Yes." He looked at her over the rim of his glass with amusement in his eyes.

"Clearly you would have made an excellent spy because getting information out of you is torture."

Graham chuckled. "Tell me how you like the steak."

Alexis rolled her eyes then cut into her steak. She took a bite and actually hummed in pleasure. She chewed slowly to savor every morsel. "Oh my…" she was finally able to manage. "If you ever give up the educational profession you have a career as a chef."

He chuckled. "I'd thought about it once or twice."

"I can see why," she muttered, talking around her food. "Is that Wynton Marsalis playing?"

"You have a good ear."

"I have a lot of his music. But I don't think I've heard this one before. I just recognize his intonations."

"It's from one of his early recordings."

She slowly bobbed her head to the music while sipping her wine. She set her glass down. "You seem to have quite a repertoire—navy pilot, multilingual, talented cook, well-read, educated, well traveled…"

He slid out of his seat, picked up their dishes and put them in the sink. He refilled their glasses. "I think you're leaving something out."

"Hmm, what might that be?"

"That I'm at my best when I'm making love to you." He stared right into her soul.

Warmth flooded through her as if she'd slipped into a hot tub.

His lids lowered a bit over his eyes giving them a smoldering look. He reached out and ran the tip of his finger along her jaw and then up across her bottom lip.

She held her breath.

"Do you dance?" he asked so quietly that she nearly

missed his question, which took her completely off guard.

She blinked back her surprise. "Um, yes."

"Good." He took her hand, helped her down off the stool and led her to the center of the room.

A classic Nancy Wilson tune was playing softly, "Tonight May Have to Last Me All My Life." He pulled her close and effortlessly glided and swayed with her across the floor. The feeling of being held in his arms like this was as sensual as foreplay. Their bodies moved as one, the music swelled, the words mesmerized.

Alexis closed her eyes and rested her head on his chest. The steady beat of his heart underscored the rhythm and pulse of Nancy's voice.

She wished she had the words to explain how Graham made her feel. When he touched her it was akin to awakening from a deep and prolonged sleep and feeling alive for the very first time. Like now as his fingertips grazed her face and along the hollow of her throat causing a tremble to roll along her spine. Their dance was as much a physical concerto as it was an erotic symphony. Their movements teased and taunted and aroused until it was like the act of sex itself.

The music came to a soulful end but they continued to move together so slowly, holding each other to the tune that they'd created.

Graham dipped his head to look down at her. Alexis's eyes fluttered open, she lifted her head from his chest and in that instant that they connected she felt full, complete and awash with a joy that eclipsed anything she'd ever felt before and it terrified her.

Without a word, he took her hand and led her down the staircase to his bedroom.

Her heart thundered in her chest. She felt like she was going to a boy's room for the first time while his parents weren't home. It was scary and exhilarating all at once.

Her eyes slowly adjusted to the dimmer lighting. A king-size bed dominated the room that was another reflection of Graham's fine taste in furnishings with a distinctive masculine touch.

She figured his entire apartment must be wired for sound as she heard the faint strains of music softly enveloping them and there was no sign of a stereo system in the room.

"Let me make you more comfortable," Graham said to her. He lifted the hem of her tank top and pulled it up and over her head. He tossed in onto a side chair near the corner of the room. His eyes burned across the rise of her breasts. He lowered his head and placed a hot kiss in the valley before sliding the straps of her bra over her shoulders then unsnapping the hook in the back.

She eased out of it, letting it drop to the floor and relished in the gaze of admiration that beamed from his eyes when he looked at her.

His hands lowered to her waist and then guided her back toward his enormous bed. She plopped down on it, then scooted up to the top. He did a slow crawl on his hands and knees until he was perched above her.

"You made it very difficult for me to keep my hands off of you today," he said in a voice laced with desire.

"Did I?" she replied coyly.

He flicked his tongue across her nipple. She hissed in air through her teeth.

"Yes." He did the same to the other before drawing one into his mouth. Her back instinctively arched. Her eyes slammed shut. "And I think it was very unfair of you to be so close…" He kissed her mouth. "And still so far." His arm slid down between their bodies and his fingers found their way around the band of her running pants and began to pull them down while she helped by wiggling out of them, leaving her in just her black thong.

Graham groaned low in his throat. "I want to imagine that this is what you always wear under your clothes." He caressed the curve of her hip and down the inside of her thighs with his thumbs. Her skin fluttered beneath his fingertips. He cupped her sex in his palm and gently massaged her until she was wet with wanting.

He moved down her body, dropping hot kisses along the path of her flesh. He kissed the inside of her legs, behind her knees along her calves and back up until he reached the apex of thighs. She was hot and moist. He pressed his lips against her damp thong and gently nibbled.

She gasped. Her hips writhed. She gripped the sheets in her fists.

He delved deeper—using his tongue and his teeth— against the strip of near-sheer fabric that was more of a turn-on for them both than a barrier.

She spread her legs and bent her knees, giving herself over to him as he sought his treasure.

The intensity grew within her as his rhythm quickened. He gripped her hips to keep her from bucking too wildly, as he licked and sucked and hummed against her wet heat.

Her head spun and her heart raced so rapidly that she was sure she would pass out. The tingling and tensing of her muscles began on the bottom of her feet and crept up the back of her legs, settled and gripped her cheeks, spread across her stomach, up through her chest, out to her arms, then reversed its course and became trapped in her center, throbbing and pulsing and begging for release. He shoved his tongue inside her and the world stopped spinning. She was suspended in a vortex of unimaginable sensations that shook and shook and shook her while she screamed his name over and again and tears squeezed out of her eyes and her body jerked with jolts of pleasure.

"That's only the beginning," he murmured against her and slowly made his way up her body.

Chapter 13

Graham braced himself between her legs. He rose up on his knees, grabbed her hips firmly in his large palms and pushed deep inside her in one long, hard stroke.

All the air rushed from her lungs. *She wasn't ready. She wasn't ready.* The last wave of her orgasm still rolled through her when he entered. Her insides instantly convulsed in response, gripping him, sucking him in. There was nothing she could do to hold back the dam that was ready to burst. Their bodies had wills of their own and all they sought was satisfaction.

They moved together giving and taking, in and out, fast and slow, faster, harder, more, longer. Enough! Enough! Now. Now. *Yesss!*

"Are you okay?" Graham gently asked against the shell of her ear.

Alexis nodded, still unable to speak. Graham lightly

kissed her cheek and rolled off her and onto his back. She instantly felt bereft without the close contact. She turned onto her side and curled against him.

He smiled, threw his arm across her hip and closed his eyes.

She hadn't realized she'd fallen asleep until Graham shifted his body in the bed and she slowly rose from a deep, sweet slumber. She blinked, trying to focus in the dark. The blue light of the digital bedside clock showed 1:00 a.m. They'd actually slept for hours and even though it was truly the middle of the night she felt utterly refreshed *and* starved.

She took a quick peek at Graham and gently extricated herself from his embrace, eased out of the bed and the room. She tiptoed up the steps to the kitchen in search of a snack.

Turning on the light she went to the fridge, opened it and stepped back in shock. The restaurant-styled double-door stainless-steel refrigerator was packed from front to back, top to bottom. She blinked and blinked. Every cold item one could imagine lined the shelves.

Curious she crossed the kitchen space and opened the door of the pantry and that nearly took her breath away. The cabinets from top and bottom were also loaded. And she was sure that the deep freezer would be packed, as well.

Admittedly she'd seen the voluminous amounts of food he'd purchased at the supermarket. At the time she simply chalked it up to him not having done any food shopping due to his travel schedule. But clearly that was not the case. This was an accumulation over time. It was just so odd.

She pulled open the drawer of the vegetable bin and took out an apple. She diced it into pieces, got some peanut butter from the cabinet and spread it on the slices. She took her plate of peanut butter-coated apples and sat down at the island. She picked up one of her treats and chewed it slowly, thoughtfully. It was just so odd, she thought again. If it had been anything other than fresh, edible food, and neatly stored, he could potentially be a candidate for an episode of *Hoarders*. The show was one of her guilty pleasures. Having watched it so often she was a pseudo expert on the myriad of reasons why people keep or buy an overabundance of "stuff."

Generally, if they weren't plain crazy, the hoarding was to compensate for some loss or to fill some void. She chewed another apple slice.

The crunching of the apple muffled the sound of Graham's approach. All of a sudden he was right behind her.

"I woke up and you were gone." He kissed the back of her neck. He slid onto the stool next to her and snatched up one of the apple slices. "One of my faves."

"You, um, have a lot of food," she said, quietly emphasizing each word.

His jaw slowed. He put what was left of the apple back on the plate.

Alexis watched an array of emotions play across his face, finally settling on closed and shut down.

Graham pushed back from the counter and slowly stood. "I'm going back to bed. Be sure to turn out the lights." He turned and walked away, leaving Alexis to wonder what in the world had just happened.

* * *

When she returned to the bedroom, Graham was on his side so that his back was to her. She sat on the side of the bed.

"Would you rather that I leave?"

He inhaled deeply and expelled a long breath. "Your decision."

Her insides twisted.

"But I would rather that you didn't." He turned onto his back, tucked his hands under his head and stared up at the ceiling. "It's not something…it's complicated."

She reached out and tenderly placed her hand on his chest. "You don't have to tell me anything you don't want to."

He pressed his lips together. "We… There was never enough. Always fighting over scraps. Waking up day after bloody day with hunger pains so deep in my belly that it could never be filled."

"While you lived in England…I thought you lived with relatives."

His jaw tightened. He closed his eyes. "That's partially true. My mum shipped me off when I was two, like I said. I lived with my aunt. I didn't know until years later that she'd been lying to the family about how well she was doing. She was dirt-poor, on the dole with four kids of her own. Half the time there were no lights, no heat in winter." He slowly shook his head. "I'll never forget how cold I was. I didn't ever think I would be warm."

"Didn't your mother come to see you? Didn't she ever find out what was going on?"

"I never saw my mother again until I turned seventeen."

Her heart twisted in her chest. She remained silent

without making any further comment, not even to fill in the echoes of intermittent silence. She sensed that this revelation from Graham was a major turning point in their very new relationship. He was entrusting her with a dark part of his soul and she knew in her heart that she would never betray that trust, no matter what the ultimate outcome of their relationship.

"At least a couple of times a year I was placed in a foster home—different people, schools, environments," he said in a faraway voice. "I never knew what or who I could count on or for how long. I didn't dare form any attachments because I knew that as soon as I did they would be gone." He sighed heavily.

Alexis couldn't fathom how a mother could do that to her own flesh and blood—to her child, any child. The concept was so far removed from her own reality because of the close bond that she'd had with her mother. Of course, she knew about and had seen destructive relationships between parents and their children but that didn't make it any easier to swallow.

"You asked about my mother," he said in a voice that came from far away. Alexis held her breath. "For much of my youth I didn't know what to think. I knew my aunt wasn't my mother. She didn't love me or show me any affection." The words hung in the air and she longed to gather him in her arms and promise him that it would never hurt like that again. But the cold stiffness of his body language, the feeling that he had turned inward screamed "don't touch me, I don't need your pity," even as the ragged edge of his words seemed to say something different.

"I didn't know until years later that she'd always known what was going on. I remember going to bed at night and praying that my real mother would come and get me. She never did."

Tears stung her eyes, but she vowed that she would not cry.

"So there you have the whole sordid tale of my young, tortured life," he said, the sarcasm adding to the sting of his words. He slowly turned his head to look at her and his eyes raked over her face as if seeing her for the first time. "I've never told anyone that story before. No one other than Blake," he said, almost as if he was surprised by his own revelations.

"Thank you for trusting me," she said, softly.

He took his hand from behind his head and reached out to cup her cheek. "I think that maybe it means something, eh?"

A shadow of a smile teased her thoroughly kissed lips. "Could be the start of something."

He grinned and the light came back on in his eyes. He drew her to him. "Could be," he murmured against her mouth. "And just so that you know, I actually have Milton come up twice a month and ship most of it off to shelters and family safe houses."

She grinned. "So there's no need for an intervention."

"The only thing I need help with," he said, turning her onto her back, "is not wanting you every minute of the day."

Chapter 14

When the sun came up they both fought the urge to stay in bed and keep talking throughout the day, but that was out of the question. And although he still had not said anything to Alexis about Tracy's surprise visit, he didn't want to feed any flames by both he and Alexis being out at the same time that was not clearly business related.

Instead they got up at dawn, did a quick wash up and went jogging before returning to their own apartments to get ready for the day and made sure that they arrived separately to the office.

Alexis virtually hummed her way through her morning. She had an extra bounce in her step and a smile or a good word for everyone, and even Tracy's extra chilly attitude didn't bother her in the least during the impromptu staff meeting that she'd called. She wanted to bring everyone up to speed on the current projects, get any input or suggestions and to remind them once again that her door was always open.

When the meeting broke up, Alexis asked Tracy if she could hang behind for a few minutes. She acted as if she was going to protest, but apparently thought better of it.

She remained seated and tapped her foot impatiently while the staff filed out. Once everyone was gone, Alexis pulled up a chair and sat right in front of Tracy, so close in fact that it startled her. She blinked back her surprise.

Alexis leaned forward, stared right into her light brown eyes. "I know you have your place here and that you've worked hard to get where you are. I've read your file. You're talented. But here's the deal. I'm here now. You may not like it or like me, and that's okay. But you will respect me as I will respect you. We're both adults here so let's dispense with the eye rolling, the mumbling and snide comments. There's no room for that. I won't sit back and be undermined by the people that I work with, no matter what their title is. I'm more than happy to find a way to make it easy…or not. That's up to you."

She leaned back, never once taking her eyes off Tracy.

Tracy's throat worked up and down as if she wanted to spit something out but thought better of it. She let out a soft breath and lifted her chin.

"I'm sorry if I gave you the impression that I was being difficult." She swallowed. "It won't happen again."

Alexis knew that if Tracy had the chance to snatch her up by the collar and could get away with it, she would. Unfortunately, that option wasn't on the table. She pushed back in her chair and stood, effectively ending the tête-à-tête. "As I said, my door is always open."

Tracy forced an artificial smile. "Thank you. I appreciate that." She grabbed her belongings, spun on her heel and walked out.

Alexis's body visibly softened the moment Tracy was out of the door. She didn't like confrontations with staff, but she had no qualms about putting people in check when the need arose. It prevented bigger problems down the line. She hoped that at least from now on there would be a semblance of decorum between them.

Claire poked her head in the door. "Mr. Stone is on line two."

Her stomach fluttered. "Thanks." She waited until Claire was back at her desk. She picked up the phone. "Yes, Mr. Stone, what can I do for you?"

"You've done plenty, but I won't dwell on that." He chuckled deep in his throat and Alexis felt her cheeks heat. "I was wondering if you were free for lunch?"

"I'm sorry, I'd made plans to have lunch with Claire."

"My loss. I was going to order in…lock the door, turn off the phone…"

She giggled. "You need to stop."

"Dinner, then?"

"I think I can manage dinner. My place?"

"Can you give me the address?"

She laughed again. "Goodbye. Eight o'clock."

"Can't wait," he said before disconnecting the call.

Alexis returned the receiver to the cradle, leaned back in her seat and smiled. She could fall for him. Fall really hard. But she had to keep a clear head. The bottom line was he was still her boss. This was a work environment and the last thing she needed was the added complication of an office romance becoming a distraction for her staff, especially when she was trying to establish a rapport and a level of respect from the members of her team. All of that would be out of the window if it was thought or discovered that she was sleeping with the boss. It was a scenario that she didn't want to see played out, and she would do whatever was necessary to make sure that it didn't happen.

She returned her attention to the overview portfolios of the schools under the R.E.A.L. umbrella. In total there were twenty-five schools, sprinkled across the country with a large concentration on the East Coast. There were two in California; one in Austin, Texas; Denver, Colorado, and one on the island of Antigua. Each of them had different needs based on demographics and the composition of the student base. What she was most interested in was how the schools were initially selected and how they had improved since becoming part of the program, and then there was the flagship school that was based in Bedford-Stuyvesant in Brooklyn that started out as a storefront and was now K–8.

The progressive graphs that showed the development of the schools were pretty irrefutable. Test scores, attendance and graduation, teacher retention, parent involvement were up at all of the schools that R.E.A.L. was a part of.

Before coming on board she'd done some research but being on the inside and seeing the phenomenal effects of this program elevated her opinion of Graham and his vision.

She turned toward her door at the sound of the light tap. "Hey, Claire." She noticed she had her purse. "Wow, lunchtime already."

"If you're busy we can always reschedule."

"No. I need to get up and out. And I'm actually hungry." She put her computer to sleep, took her purse from her bottom desk drawer and walked out with Claire.

"I thought we could go to this great Ethiopian place. The food is great, they give you plenty and the service is prompt so you can actually finish a meal during the lunch hour without feeling rushed," Claire said as they exited the building.

"Sounds good to me."

They took the leisurely two-block walk as the Midtown Manhattan lunch-goers began to fill the streets and Claire pointed out some must-go places along the way: a day spa, nail salon and after-work lounge. Alexis had been to New York on many occasions, but always as a tourist. She was seeing the city through new eyes. She was now part of the energy that made the Big Apple so special.

The restaurant proved to be even better than Claire described. The decor was warm and inviting. It felt like a family neighborhood restaurant instead of one in the middle of Manhattan. The seating was huge overstuffed pillows in brilliant colors and textures beneath low tables. The aroma wafting from the kitchen was too tantalizing for words.

They were quickly shown to their seats. Claire suggested the *Doro Tibs*—a boneless chicken dish that was marinated in spices—along with *Gomen,* collard greens that had been simmered in vegetable broth and spices.

"So tell me a little bit about yourself. I've read your résumé, but tell me something that's not on paper."

Claire gave some verbal snapshots of her childhood, the youngest of three, she attended public school, and then Brooklyn College. She worked for a couple of years for the Department of Education before she heard Graham speak at a conference at the Harlem State Office Building.

"I believed in everything he was doing and was trying to do. I convinced him to take me on in any capacity. I started out in Human Resources, trained in pretty much every department on my way over and up." She smiled, then took a bite of her chicken.

"Wow. Do most of the other staff members have similar stories?"

Claire was thoughtful for a moment. "Well, the majority of the staff came from other organizations. I'm the only one that I can think of that came through the ranks. They were all hired for the positions that they're in."

"I know you confided in me before about Tracy and that she has some hard feelings about not getting my job." She took a mouthful of *Gomen*. Her eyes fluttered in delight. "I haven't brought it up with Mr. Stone, but what are your thoughts? I've pretty much gotten the cold shoulder since I arrived. I know the job is part of it but I get the sense that it's more than that."

For the first time Claire looked uncomfortable. She kept her focus on her food. She kind of shrugged and gave an abbreviated shake of her head.

"If you're uncomfortable, I don't want to put you in an awkward position."

Claire finally looked up. "I... There were rumors that something was going on between Tracy and Mr. Stone."

Alexis's heart nearly stopped. *Graham and Tracy.*

"I never believed it. Mr. Stone isn't like that. But the rumors started because...they seemed so close. You know. They worked late nights, traveled together." She sighed. "But then the rumors faded away, the organization grew." She gave a tight smile.

That sick feeling that had settled in her stomach like a lead weight slowly eased. Rumors. That's all. Nothing to it. This was all the more reason why no one would ever say the same thing about her. She shifted the conversation to the early days of the organization and where it was now. They shared brief stories about their life growing up, Alexis in Atlanta and Claire in Queens, NY. She liked Claire. Not only was she a stellar assistant, she was a really nice young woman.

They returned from lunch and the day marched on at its usual breakneck pace. Before she realized it, six o'clock was rolling around and the offices were emptying out. As busy as she'd remained for the balance of the day she couldn't shake off what Claire had said about Graham and Tracy. What if it was true? What if that was the real reason behind the animosity—the failed relationship? Perhaps Tracy saw her as not only a threat regarding the job but a replacement for Graham's affections.

She couldn't broach the subject with Graham. To do so would break the pseudo confidence between her and Claire and she supposed the real reason for her consternation was, what if he lied to her? Would she know for sure?

Chapter 15

Graham and Alexis had fallen into a comfortable routine. They'd generally have an early dinner at one or the other's apartment, go for a run and spend the night together. It was so easy and felt so right. They simply fit together mentally and physically.

But tonight, Alexis begged off, saying that she was really tired, wanted to make some calls and turn in early—for a change—she'd added with a smile. Graham reluctantly agreed to a night without her. At the root of it she wasn't sure if she could keep from saying something to him about Tracy. She needed a bit of distance and some girl talk to get her head straight.

After their run and a quick, but passionate parting kiss in the elevator, Alexis took a long hot bath while her dinner warmed in the oven. By the time she finished eating and cleaning up the kitchen, it was nearing eight-thirty. She didn't want to call Naomi while she was trying to get April ready for bed, but she also didn't want to wait too long and wake her if she dozed off. Maybe she'd luck out and it would be Brice's night to take care of the baby.

She propped herself up against the plump pillows on her bed and speed-dialed Naomi. Naomi picked up on the third ring, sounding remarkably bright and alert.

"Lexi! How are you? What's been going on?"

Just hearing her best friend's voice made her feel better. She settled against her pillows. "I'm good, girl. What about you and my goddaughter and your gorgeous husband?"

"We are all fine. Tonight is Brice's night." She giggled. "I'm curled on the living room couch, sipping a glass of white wine and watching one of these crazy-ass Housewives shows. They actually pay people for this foolishness."

They both laughed.

"So what's going on? We haven't talked lately. How is the job? And the sexy boss?"

"Well…I can tell you because you know me and you know the kind of woman I am…"

"Lexi." She dragged the name out. "What happened?"

Alexis took a breath. "I… We slept together."

There was a moment of silence on the line. "Humph, as much as I was hoping against it," Naomi finally said, "I had a feeling that was gonna happen. Well, girl, you done spilled the beans now. I want details, details and don't you dare leave anything out!"

Alexis crossed her legs at the ankles. "Well, we took a trip to D.C.…."

About a half hour later Alexis had brought Naomi up

to date, including the revelation made by Claire about Graham and Tracy.

"So there you have it," Alexis finally said.

"Wow, sis, I'm at a loss."

"That's helpful," she droned.

Naomi blew out a breath. "After all the hot sex and great conversations and the wonderful working partnership, at the end of the day he's still your boss, Lexi. More than likely things will go great between you, but…"

"I know…what if it doesn't."

"What if what Claire said is true and it's part of Graham's M.O.?"

"I can't believe that. He doesn't come across that way."

"Are you sure or has he simply got your panties all twisted?"

Inwardly she laughed, thinking about the extra panties that she kept in her bottom drawer. "Both," she readily admitted.

"All I can say is don't let it interfere with your work or with how you interact with your staff. It could get messy."

"I know," she said quietly. "I've never known a man like him," she said in a voice reserved for a confessional. "He's everything I've ever wanted."

"Wow. That's a first. I don't think I've ever heard you say that about a man. Ian was close, but…wow."

Alexis felt all fluttery inside. She'd never confessed to feeling that way about a man, to herself or anyone else.

"Don't think for a minute that I am trying to throw cold water on you, it would just sizzle anyway, but I do want you to be happy, Lexi. You deserve it. And it's long overdue. Maybe Graham is the one, ya know."

"Maybe."

"Take your time. You'll know if he's Mr. Right or Mr. Right Now."

"How?"

"When you wake up in the morning and your first thought is of him. When you get that funny feeling in the center of your chest whenever you think about him. When he steps into a room it seems as if the lights finally came on and you feel safe and secure when you are with him. All your doubts and fears shift to the background and are replaced with…joy. And you can't imagine him not being in your life."

Alexis took that all in. She listened to those words play in her head over and over until she began to drift asleep and an instant before she slipped off into a perfect slumber she thought, *Mr. Right*.

Alexis arrived at the office the following morning with the conversation between her and Naomi still playing loudly in her head.

The big question that she could not escape was, how did she let herself get in so deep and so quickly with Graham? It was like her crazed romantic alter ego had taken over her mind and body, like some sci-fi movie. What continued to give her pause was that she knew deep in her soul that it was more than good sex. That's what scared her. Graham had inadvertently awakened a part of her that didn't want it any other way.

"Good morning."

The two words in that sexy British timbre snatched her breath away. Gingerly she put down her cup of coffee so as not to spill it all over her desk. Her heart jumped then settled to an almost normal rhythm.

Damn he was fine. Tall and slender with the muscle tone of an athlete, smooth milk-chocolate complexion and the most piercing dark eyes that devoured her after boring into her soul, showcased beneath sweeping thick brows with lashes that women would pay for. *But his mouth*. Oh, Lawd.

Alexis cleared her throat. "Good morning." She offered up her best smile.

"Mind if I come in?" he said from the doorway.

"You're the boss."

If she wasn't mistaken she would have sworn that he flinched at her offhand comment.

He strolled into her airspace and she grew so warm she felt as if she would self-combust. She followed his pantherlike prowl until he took a seat next to her desk.

Graham leaned a bit toward her. She caught a whiff of his scent. Her bud twitched between her legs.

"I missed you last night," he said on a whisper that made the hairs on her arms rise.

Alexis sucked in a short breath and tried to swallow over the dryness in her throat. "I'm sure you found something to occupy your time." She tried to hold his gaze but she couldn't and casually reached for her cell phone and made a slight show of checking for any missed text messages. The moment's reprieve got her head back in the game.

"What would you say if I told you that I didn't want anything or anyone else to occupy my time?"

"I think I'll refrain from saying anything and stay out of trouble."

"You see—" he subtly reached over and ran his finger across her knuckles "—when I'm left alone like I was last night I have nothing but time on my hands to think about all the trouble I intend to get into with you." His lashes lowered halfway over his eyes.

What she wanted to do was jump up out of her seat, grab him by his starched collar and have her way with him right in the chair where he sat.

She lightly ran her tongue across her lips. "Hmm, Mr. Stone, I do believe you have too much time on your hands."

"Exactly. And I want to be sure that you change that. Tonight." He pushed up from his seat.

She arched a brow, leaned back and folded her arms. "Is that right?" she challenged.

"Yes. Do you think you can?" he tossed right back at her.

Her eyes darkened. A smug smile tugged at her mouth. "I'll let you be the judge of that, Mr. Stone."

"Looking forward to it." He turned and strolled out of the door.

Alexis released a long, hot breath. It was as if her nerve endings had been overstimulated and all he did was talk to her, brush his finger across her knuckles and she was on fire. Yet, she still knew it was more than the sexual string that he was able to pull. It was the whole package.

She sucked on her bottom lip in thought. She had to keep it cool and professional. There were no guarantees about where this would go and she wasn't going to let her hormones rule her head. But in the meantime…she reached into her bottom desk drawer and retrieved her extra panties and went to change before heading to her off-site meetings.

Her first meeting was at R.E.A.L. Downtown, located in Brooklyn, for students K–5. She wasn't sure what to expect, but whatever ideas she may have had meant nothing after seeing the program in operation.

First, the building was spotless. It was a renovated brick building that sat on the corner of Henry Street on a tree-lined block surrounded by shops, private homes and plenty of transportation. St. Francis College was nearby as well as Packer Collegiate, Brooklyn Friends School and NYU Poly. R.E.A.L. Downtown was clearly in good company.

After checking in at the front desk, she met with the head of school, Ms. Daniels, who had been with the program since it began five years earlier.

"It's amazing what we do here. The children inspire me to be a better educator," she said. "I've worked in private schools as well as public, and by far this is my most life-affirming experience. The concept is global," she said as they walked out to the back of the building.

Alexis was stunned to see a blooming, vibrant fruit and vegetable garden that rivaled any she'd ever seen and it was being tended to by students.

Two groups were present. One group was listening to a talk on gardening, the other group was pruning, watering and picking and no one was older than ten.

"Is this part of the curriculum?"

"Absolutely. It's part of their life. They get to see the vegetables and fruit grow from seeds. They take care of everything and usually once per month, the parents come in and 'shop.'"

"Impressive."

Ms. Daniels led them back inside. "The first floor has the classrooms. No more than ten students per class."

"I imagine that you have an incredibly long waiting list."

She gave a short chuckle. "Long fails to describe it. Unfortunately ninety percent of families that apply will never get in. Not because we don't want them, but we don't have the room or the staff."

Alexis blew out a frustrated sigh.

"Down here is our creative arts department. We do everything with the children from music and dance classes, drawing, pottery making, to singing. Our reading and movie room is over here." They peeked in through the half glass door. "During the week each of the classes come in and listen to a reading by a teacher or a guest, or they can read a book out loud from something that they have selected from the library, or they can create their own stories as a group. On Friday, we have movie day, complete with popcorn."

They walked to the end of the hall and took the stairs up one flight. "Here are the more formal classrooms."

Each of the ten rooms had Smart Boards and computer stations. There were images being flashed on the board while the teacher spoke to her enthralled students.

"We all have breakfast and lunch together in the school cafeteria in the basement. And they have an afternoon snack, usually fruit."

"Where was this school when I was growing up?" Alexis said.

Ms. Daniels laughed. "I know what you mean. I feel the same way." They returned to her office.

"I am beyond impressed," Alexis said. "It's one thing to see it on paper but it's quite another to witness it first hand."

"Mr. Stone's vision is our vision, Ms. Montgomery. Anyone who is a part of this mission understands that and so do the parents. Parent participation is part of our success. We insist on parent engagement. Attendance at the quarterly PTA meetings is a must. Volunteering, donating, sitting in on classes…parents are involved."

Alexis nodded. "So, with all that being said, what do you need? What more would you like to see here?"

"I wouldn't necessarily want to see more students in our building. That would greatly impact our effectiveness, unless we expand with more space and more teachers. What I would like to see is another school like this one in the community. There are so many needy kids out there."

Alexis stood and extended her hand. "Thank you so much for your time, Ms. Daniels. You are doing an incredible job here. These children are very lucky."

Alexis's trip uptown to Harlem took about forty minutes, but the ride on the fabled A train was worth every minute of it. She couldn't help but wonder why the train was so crowded in the middle of the afternoon. Where in the world was everyone going?

She arrived at R.E.A.L. Harlem on One Hundred Twentieth and Amsterdam blocks from Columbia University. This location was middle school through grade twelve. It was a former six-story turn-of-the-century apartment building that had been renovated, and was the first "green" school building in the area.

This was a far cry from anything she'd ever seen before in terms of setup and design for a school. It looked more like a think tank for Apple or Google. There were a row of classrooms along one wall. It was an open floor plan concept, in what would have otherwise been the wide hallway, with beanbag seating, overstuffed pillows, circular chairs and low tables. Young people were everywhere in the open space, engaged in a variety of projects, listening to lectures in small conversational groups, studying or working at computer stations.

The head of school, Mr. Fleming, gave her a tour of the six floors, which included classrooms, more open seating, two cafeterias, labs, a gym, a state-of-the-art theater, and a video and audio editing suite. There was a maximum student body of 350. Since the school had opened, its first and only graduating class to date had all received either partial or full scholarships to some of the best colleges in the nation, and the next graduating class was on track to do the same.

Mr. Fleming attributed the success of the school to small class size, committed teachers and parents, and innovation in teaching.

When Alexis left and was returned home she was more committed than ever to ensuring that Graham's vision was realized.

Seeing what she saw and knowing more now than she knew before, and understanding that all of this brilliance was the brainchild of one man was such a serious turn-on she couldn't wait to get home, take her clothes off for him and get wrapped up in his arms. Brilliance and caring for others—especially young people—was a crazy aphrodisiac for her. There was nothing hotter than a sexy man with brains *and* a good heart.

Chapter 16

"When are you heading back out of town?" Graham asked. He picked up his mug of beer and took a swallow. The hum of conversation at the local after-work bar buzzed around them.

"Looks like the end of the week. I'll be going to D.C. for a few days and then out to Phoenix for a conference. Then I'll be back." Blake scooped up some peanuts from the bowl, tossed his head back and dropped them in. He chewed thoughtfully. "I'm probably going to slow down a bit on the traveling."

Graham angled his head toward his friend. "Oh, yeah, why?"

Blake was a bit slow to answer. "If she'll have me, I plan to ask Sydni to marry me. Not right away. But soon."

Graham nearly spilled his beer. "Whoa! What?"

Blake chuckled a bit from nerves and relief after actually having said the words out loud.

"I had no idea it was like that with you and Sydni. I mean I know you two were kind of seeing each other but…damn, man, you sure can keep a secret."

"It kind of hit me like that, too. I mean we've been seeing each other off and on for about a year now. But we are never in one place long enough to make a real go of it."

Graham hummed in agreement.

"I've been thinking about it for a while. In the end I always arrive at the same place. I want to be with her."

"Be with her enough that you want to spend the rest of your life with her or be with her enough to get through a full week together?"

"Very funny."

"But very real. The day to day is a whole different ball game. You two don't even live in the same city."

Blake nodded his head. "Which is the reason why I'm moving to New Orleans at the end of the month."

Graham's eyes widened. He opened his mouth but no words came out.

"It's the first step. I know it seems out of the blue but, yeah, I do want to be sure. The first step is to at least be in the same city. My job is mobile. She is second in line at her father's company with headquarters in Louisiana. I couldn't ask her to leave. I wouldn't."

Graham didn't know what to say. He was still trying to process the idea that his mate was planning on getting married, and now the added surprise of his moving out of New York. "So you haven't asked her yet," he said, finally finding his voice.

Blake shook his head, no.

"How do you know she will even say yes?"

"I don't. But I know that I'm in love with her, man, and that she loves me and if we had a chance we could make it work. I'm willing to take that chance."

Graham was silent for a moment. "I hear you, brotha." He shook his head and grinned. "I never thought I'd hear those words come out of your mouth. She must be some kind of special to get the kid to slow down."

Blake laughed. "No one could be more surprised than me. I wake up and all I think about is talking to her, seeing her. I wonder what she's doing during the day…"

Graham listened mildly amused as his good buddy waxed poetic about his feelings for Sydni even as his gut slowly began to twist. He'd experienced those same feelings about Alexis. His jaw clenched. But that was different. That wasn't love, it was sex. Good sex and nothing more. And good sex didn't translate into love and marriage. Besides, he wasn't the marrying kind. There wasn't a woman out there that would ever be able to fill all the holes that had been dug out of his heart and soul. Not even Alexis Montgomery.

So that night and all the nights that followed, even while he moved deep inside her and listened to her cry out his name and felt overcome with something he couldn't put a name to, he kept reminding himself it was only good sex and nothing more.

"I have to go to L.A. for a few days," Graham said as they jogged along First Avenue.

"Yes, I saw it on your schedule."

They turned the corner onto their street.

"I was hoping you'd come with me."

Her heart jumped and not from running. She took a quick glance at him. The conversation that she'd had with Claire weeks earlier played back in her head. She was building a strong rapport with her staff. Although Tracy remained stiff and aloof, they were at least cordial. The last thing she needed at this important crossroads in her position with the company was for rumors to start flying. She would lose all credibility and without her self-respect she would have nothing.

"I'd love to," she said as they came to a slow stop in front of 10 Sutton. "But I can't. Or rather, I won't."

Glen opened the front door and they walked in wiping their faces with the towels that they had hanging around their necks.

Graham literally stabbed the elevator button. He waited until the doors had closed behind them. He turned to her. "Why won't you?"

She looked up at him and for an instant she couldn't remember why she wouldn't go with him anywhere he wanted. "Graham, it's the middle of the week. When you're not there, I'm the next one in line. There would be no good reason for the both of us to go. It would only give the staff something to talk about and I don't want that."

He placed his hand on her waist. "We were together in D.C.," he said, his eyes darkening with the lusty memories.

"D.C. was different. This trip isn't even business related. You're taking some vacation days for a naval reunion."

"No one has to know that we're going together."

She tilted her head to the side and gave him an "oh really" look.

He chuckled. "All right, all right, I get it. Not this time but next time." The doors opened on her floor. "I'll be down in about an hour. I have some calls to make first."

"Sure." She kissed him lightly on the lips and stepped off the elevator.

As she stood under the beat of the shower she wondered again for the countless time what she was doing being involved with Graham. She was in a relationship that she couldn't talk about to anyone other than her closest friend. She couldn't really be seen with her lover in public. He didn't seem as if he had any intention of it becoming anything more than what it was. Where was it all going? And why was she still in it? She had a sinking feeling that it was all going to explode all over the both of them and not in a good way.

The question, *why am I still in it,* played in the background of her thoughts, even as she wrapped her legs around Graham's back and raised her pelvis to meet his demanding thrusts and listened to him whisper in her ear about how good she made him feel, that he didn't want anyone else, how beautiful and important she was, while his body emptied into hers and shuddered with release, and they held each other and kissed and laughed and talked well into the night; *that is why,* she reasoned as the sun began to rise over the Manhattan skyline and she studied the outline of his body beneath her sheets. She'd rather be with Graham, under whatever circumstances they could manage, than to be with anyone else.

The three days and then the weekend that Graham was in California were the longest five days of Alexis's life. The office seemed to have lost its sparkle without his presence. She lost count of how often she would check her cell phone during the day for any messages from him and how her heart would sing when there were. But her nights were the most unbearable. Loneliness couldn't begin to describe how she felt as she tossed and turned in her big empty bed.

Her only ray of sunshine was that she'd planned to visit Naomi in Virginia for the Fourth of July holiday. Planning for her mini-getaway and seeing her goddaughter for the first time in months was just the medicine she needed to purge Graham, temporarily, out of her system.

"I'm going to fly down. It's an hour flight and although I love taking the train, I don't want half of my time away to be taken up by traveling."

"Makes sense. Getting away will do you good," Graham said, over the roar of loud male laughter in the background.

"Sounds like you're having a ball."

He laughed. "These guys are crazy. But it's great to see everyone," he shouted over the noise. "I miss you."

Her heart nearly stopped. She wasn't sure she'd heard him with all of the whooping and hollering in the background. Someone was calling him in all the chaos of sound. "What did you say?"

"Gotta go, luv, duty calls. I'll try to catch you before you leave."

"Sure. Enjoy."

"You, too."

The call disconnected. Slowly she put the cell phone down on the bed. Maybe she'd only imagined that he'd said that he missed her. In the months that they'd been seeing each other they'd never shared any words of commitment *or* intent. So maybe she simply needed to hear something so badly that she only imagined that she heard him say that he missed her. Her eyes stung for a moment. This was why this relationship was so very wrong. She pounded her fist into the mattress.

Chapter 17

"I cannot believe how big this baby has gotten," Alexis said as she marveled at her goddaughter. "You used to be a little chicken nugget, a chicken nugget," she repeated in that voice that adults take on when they talked to infants. She nibbled on her toes, which brought on heart-warming baby laughter.

"Four months has flown by," Naomi said. "I see her every day and I can't believe how much she grows and changes in the blink of an eye."

The two friends sat out on Naomi's back porch taking in the warming rays of the fading sun. As soon as the sun was down the fireworks display would begin in earnest. In the distance one could hear the pop of firecrackers and see the intermittent bursts of color that would shoot toward the heavens.

Alexis leaned back in her chair and quietly sipped on her glass of iced tea.

"You know I love you, right?"

Alexis blinked and turned her attention to Naomi. "Yeah, girl, and right back at ya."

"And you know I love having you here."

Alexis slowly put her glass down on the circular table that separated them. "Yes," she said warily.

"You want to tell me the real reason why you're here and not with Graham on a long holiday weekend?"

Her stomach rose and fell. "It's a long uninteresting story."

"I'm interested and we have plenty of time. What's going on?"

Alexis looked away. She pushed out a long sigh. "Outside of the bedroom our relationship doesn't exist," she finally said and the out-loud admission shook her to her core.

Naomi was quiet for a while. "Do you really believe that?" she gently asked.

Alexis's throat was on fire. Her eyes clouded with water. "It's true. We are never seen in public together unless it's business. We jog together in the evening but that's about it. We've never been on a date. We don't hold hands. We can't acknowledge our relationship at work." She bit down on the inside of her bottom lip to keep it from trembling. "This isn't me, Naomi." She turned pained eyes on her friend. "I'm not used to living in the shadows. I feel like a mistress or worse a 'side piece.'"

"Aw, Lexi, you know better than that."

"Do I? I don't know what I know when it comes to him that's the problem."

"I'm going to ask you something and you're not going

to like it but I need you to answer me. Why are you in a relationship that doesn't reflect you being treated like the amazing woman that you are? Are you afraid that if you tell him how you feel, you'll lose him?"

Her throat worked up and down. She blinked away the water in her eyes. "Yes," she finally managed.

"If you didn't care about him it wouldn't matter if you lost him or not," Naomi said, softly. "Would it?" The wise words hit Alexis right between the eyes.

"What are you saying?"

"I'm saying that maybe it's time that you admit how you really feel about him and tell him. Put your cards on the table. It's the only way you'll ever know if he's worth it."

"Listen to you giving me advice," she playfully chastised, "Ms. Pretending-to-be-someone-else. Where did you tell Brice you worked when you met? What did you tell him you did for a living?"

Naomi huffed. "Now, you know that was a whole different ball game. Besides, if I remember correctly that whole ruse was *your* brilliant idea. And it wasn't until he knew the truth that we were able to have a real relationship."

"That man was crazy about you. He wouldn't have cared if you told him you were a circus clown. He would have still been all over you."

Naomi giggled. "Don't try to change the subject," she said, wagging a finger at Alexis. "How do you feel about him?" she asked softly.

Alexis looked at her friend from beneath her lashes. She gazed up at the heavens and slowly shook her head. "Hooked. I can't breathe when I think about him. I can barely get through my days until it's time to see him at night. My insides feel all gooey whenever I hear his name or when he walks into a room." She scrunched up her face. "And did I ever tell you that I have to keep extra panties in my desk drawer?" Naomi bit back a laugh. "I feel like I was tossed out to sea without a life raft whenever we don't spend the night in the same bed. I live for our moments together." She released a breath. "It sounds crazy."

"It sounds more like love."

Alexis flashed her a look and rapidly shook her head in denial. "No," she said, emphatically.

Naomi shrugged. "If you say so. But trust me, I know love when I hear it."

On the short flight back to New York from Virginia, Alexis reflected on Naomi's words. Naomi had always been a straight shooter. She never did do well with deception and subterfuge, which was why the entire masquerade with Brice was a near disaster—although Alexis did think that her plan had been brilliant.

Clearly she wasn't in love with Graham. That part was ridiculous. She didn't care what Naomi thought or that she was generally always right. If anything Alexis's ego stung because she wasn't used to the whole cloak and dagger routine.

And even though her relationship with Ian wasn't on the front page of the *Atlanta Journal-Constitution*, everyone pretty much knew that they were seeing each other. They were simply discreet as they should have been in the workplace. In addition to which she and Ian were peers, equals. Graham was her boss and their relationship could be perceived in all manner of inappropriate ways. Most important, he represented a business that strove for excellence in their services and in their employees. The members of the staff were role models for the kids and she was the face of the business. She wouldn't jeopardize that, not even for her own happiness.

She wanted to be with him. That was very clear to her, she thought as she unpacked and prepared to settle down for the night. She understood the rules when she got in bed with him. And until something drastically changed she would find a way to deal with it or walk away.

As she lay in bed on her first night home from her visit with Naomi she barely slept, waiting for the tell-tale ping to alert her that a text had arrived, or the ring-tone that she'd set for his calls. By morning she was bleary-eyed and realized with a start that Graham hadn't called. She checked her cell phone twice just to make sure when the realization set in that he hadn't bothered to call her, text her, nothing. He was probably home right above her and hadn't bothered to pick up a phone to say he was back.

She vacillated between hurt and anger as she stomped out of bed and went to turn on the shower full-blast, nearly drowning out the chimes on her front door.

She halted her mini-tantrum and listened more care-fully. Yep, that was her front door. She pulled the belt of her robe tighter around her waist and went upstairs to the front door, knowing that it was Milton bringing her dry cleaning as he always did.

Alexis pulled the door open and her heart and stom-ach momentarily seemed to switch places.

"I missed my flight. Had to take the red-eye. Didn't want to call and wake you. Just got in."

Alexis tried to take it all in. He still had his luggage at his feet. He hadn't even gone to his own apartment yet. She worked hard at containing the joy that wanted to leap out of her soul and all over him.

"Come in. Come in. I'll fix some coffee."

"Ahh, sounds great."

Her heart hammered in her chest as he walked past her and inside. All the awful things she was thinking flew right out of the window.

"So besides the delay with your flight, how was your trip?" She took out the coffee from the cabinet, poured two scoopfuls in the filter, added the water and turned on the coffeemaker.

Graham came up behind her, nuzzled the back of her neck and slid his arms around her waist. She held her breath as the thrill of his touch scurried through her.

"As much fun as it was to see the fellas again, all I kept thinking about was this…" He kissed her behind her ear and slowly stroked her hips beneath the thin, silky fabric before sliding his fingers beneath the folds of her robe.

She drew in a sharp breath and turned around into his arms, looked up into his eyes and felt as if she was being pulled under water by a powerful riptide.

Graham held her chin in his palm and slowly lowered his head until the world disappeared and his mouth touched down on hers. He groaned deep in his throat and drew her fully against him. His kiss was a mixture of passion and raw need fired by an urgency that was almost frightening in its intensity.

He pulled her robe from her body and hungrily rained hot kisses along her exposed flesh, teasing her nipples with his tongue and teeth before journeying south, pausing for a moment on her fluttering stomach before placing smoldering kisses along her thighs.

She gripped his shoulders and bit down on her lip to keep from screaming.

His tongue licked her like ice cream on a cone. Her legs trembled. Graham groaned, sucking and nibbling.

The muscles in her stomach knotted and released. Her breathing hitched. She was so wet and so turned on she could have spun like a top.

They began as soft whimpers, pushed up from her throat, and continued to escalate as Graham made a delectable meal of her and he wouldn't stop until he had devoured every morsel.

Her thighs trembled over her weakened knees. Waves of pleasure flowed through her. The beat began and thumped and thumped until she was consumed by it and her only recourse was to give in and let it take her on a morning ride of ecstasy.

"Welcome back…" she said breathlessly, resting her weight against the counter. Her heart was still pounding as if she'd run a mile.

Graham stepped away, leaned on the island and eyed her lustfully. "I'll take that coffee now," he said with a smile fluttering around that incredible mouth.

Alexis's eyes sparked with laughter. She turned and took down two mugs from the cupboard and poured coffee in each. She took the half and half from the fridge. "Sugar?"

"Thanks."

They sat next to each other at the counter, sipping their coffee and stealing intermittent looks at each other.

"How was your trip to see your friend…Naomi?"

"Had a great time. I don't think I realized how much I missed her until I saw her again." She gazed off wistfully. "And the baby has gotten so big in a matter of a few months. It's amazing. Naomi has a great life, wonderful husband, beautiful baby, a home and a career waiting for her. The makings for a romance novel."

Graham studied her contemplative expression. "What about you? Do you think you have a great life?"

She blinked and looked at him. In a flash of images she envisioned that the scenario that she spoke of was actually she and Graham with a home together and a child to love.

When she focused again Graham was staring at her with his head tilted to the side waiting for her response.

She brought the coffee cup to her mouth. "Of course. I have a wonderful life," she said before taking a sip and burying her gaze in the hot brew. "What about you?" Her heart banged.

He shrugged slightly. "I couldn't ask for more. When I look back on where I came from to where I am now... I'm totally satisfied."

As much as she'd hoped he would say something else, she knew better. Graham Stone had carved his path and he had no intention of veering off of it, and there was no point in her fantasizing that what they had was anything more than what it was—great sex between consenting adults. But as much as she knew that to be true—in her head—she couldn't get her heart to go along with it. And the longer they were together, the more they talked and laughed and made love, the more difficult it was for her to ignore her heart.

Over the ensuing weeks of summer they spent all of their free time together. They jogged, took in a concert at the park, a ferry ride on Saturday along the Hudson, brunch at the local restaurant on Sunday. They were, for all intents and purposes, a couple except that it was something that was not acknowledged between them or to the world.

So Alexis was totally unprepared when Graham asked her to spend the Labor Day weekend with him at Sag Harbor.

Chapter 18

"So...are you going to go?" Naomi asked.

Alexis slowly paced her bedroom with the phone tucked between her shoulder and her ear. "I told him I'd think about it."

"What exactly are you thinking about?"

Alexis blew out a breath. "The last time he asked me to go away with him it was totally out of the question. But this time the office will be closed, no one would be aware that we were together."

"Okay. I hear a but."

"But what does it mean? I feel like the mistress that is sneaking off with the married man."

"Then don't go. Look—" she paused "—getting involved with your boss was a decision that you made. You understood the downside of it. You didn't go into this with your eyes closed. And from what you've told me he's never led you to believe anything other than what it is—two people that are attracted to each other. This trip may give you the opportunity to see him and your relationship in a completely different light."

"That's what I'm afraid of."

"Got everything?" Graham asked as he put their bags in the back of his Navigator.

"Yep." Alexis put on her sunglasses against the glare of the early-morning sun.

"Let's be on our way, then." He pulled the door open for her, helped her up, then rounded the ride and got in behind the wheel.

Surprisingly the roads weren't too bad considering that it was a holiday weekend. They listened to music, pointed out sights along the way and shared the easy banter that always flowed between them.

In no time they were pulling up to The Port in Sag Harbor.

"Reservation for Stone," Graham said to the receptionist at the front desk.

She did a quick search on the computer. "Yes, here you are. Two nights, correct, Mr. Stone?"

"Yes."

"I'll need your credit card."

He took his card out of his wallet and handed it over. She took his information, handed him back his card, keys to the cottage and a brochure of the amenities at The Port. "I'll have someone show you to your cottage. You'll be in number 10 at the end of the lane."

"Great. Thank you."

She talked into her headset and moments later a young man showed up.

"Do you have a car and luggage?" he asked.

"Yes, we're parked in the lot."

"Okay. Well, follow me." He led them to his golf cart. "We can put your luggage in here and you two can hop aboard or you can follow me in your car."

Graham gave Alexis a quick look. "We'll follow you."

They got into his Navigator and followed the golf cart along the sloping hills and smooth winding trails until they came to number 10.

The Port, which was owned by Lincoln Davenport and his wife Desiree, was a collection of cottages that dotted a tree-lined landscape just off the shore. Virtually from each of the cottages there was a view of the water. The cottages came equipped with one or two bedrooms, a full kitchen, living room and patio. The main building had a restaurant and bar, spa and massage center, pool and outdoor lounge.

The driver brought their bags into the cottage and showed them around. Graham gave him a nice tip before he left.

"This is beautiful," Alexis said, duly impressed as she walked around and took in the high-end furnishings and fixtures, and the view from the back deck was breathtaking.

"Nicer than I remember."

"You've been here before?"

"A couple of years ago." He opened the closet door in the bedroom.

She suddenly imagined him here with another woman for a quick getaway. Her stomach twisted. She shook the image aside and began to unpack.

"I should have asked, but do you swim or just look gorgeous in a bathing suit." He grinned mischievously.

She glanced up from unpacking. "Both."

Graham chuckled. "Want to go for a swim or walk around or just relax?"

"Let's walk around, and maybe go for a swim a little later."

"This is your weekend, luv," he said, walking up to her and putting his arms around her waist. "Whatever you want," he said softly, then kissed her tenderly on the lips.

If only she could believe that, she thought but didn't say.

They spent the next few hours touring the grounds, enjoying the wonderful breeze blowing off of the water before they headed over to the restaurant for lunch.

It was *so* easy and *so* good. It was the way a relationship should be. In every way they fit. They enjoyed the same things, they understood each other, laughed at the same jokes, enjoyed the same music, were athletic, they both had a passion for their work and for each other. A perfect mix—*almost,* she thought as they sat out on the back deck, sipping mojitos and watching the sun set over the water. And when they made love that first night with the full moon the only light illuminating their bedroom, and the distant sound of the ocean rushing against the shore and the almost painful tenderness with which Graham moved within her, she knew that this was what she wanted—this man, the whole package and if she couldn't have it she was going to have to do what she should have done a long time ago—let him go.

The next two days of their getaway, Alexis chose not to allow her acceptance of her feelings for Graham to interfere with their glorious weekend at The Port. They

swam, hiked, went into town and shopped, had mas-
sages at the spa and discovered that the spa was run by
Layla Lawson, Rafe's cousin by marriage. At night they
strolled along the beach and made love until the sun rose.

It was the return ride back to the city that made Alexis
realize more than ever that what they had was a make-
believe world. Under ordinary circumstances it wouldn't
have mattered, she would have simply gone along with
the program until she grew bored. This time her feelings
had gotten all tangled up in the relationship. That was
an element that she had not bargained for when she got
involved with Graham and now it was taking an emo-
tional toll that she had not been prepared to deal with.

When they returned, they easily slid back into their
comfortable existence and Alexis tried to push aside her
feelings of misgivings, her growing feelings for Graham.
But she couldn't. Graham had given her no indication
that he wanted more than what they had—something
on the side. And she refused to initiate that conversation. She wouldn't allow herself to be viewed as needy
or clingy or desperate or not mature enough to play this
very adult game.

But every time he said her name, looked at her during a meeting, fixed her a meal, kissed her—that pact
that she'd made with herself was getting more difficult
to keep.

Fortunately with the summer all but a distant memory, and school back in session, she was so busy she
barely had time to think about anything. Her days were
filled with meetings, site visits and managing the vari-
ous departments. It began to get easier to make an excuse
why she wouldn't spend the night with Graham or go

for a run. Their loving was still just as earth-shattering when they did get together, but they were getting fewer and further apart.

Now that she was more acclimated with the city, she did things on her own; visited museums, the theater, bookstores, shopped, she even went to a few movies and joined a Pilates class. The more she kept herself occupied, the easier it was to stay away from Graham. What hurt her, however, was that he never pressed, never questioned, never challenged the change in the dynamics of their relationship. That's what kept her up at night and sat like a rock in the pit of her stomach.

It was the week of Thanksgiving and Graham had magnanimously decided to close the office for the entire week instead of the two days. Alexis was actually glad for the extra time off. She'd been more tired than usual and was looking forward to relaxing and putting her feet up.

She'd been home for about an hour when her front doorbell rang. Frowning, she went to answer the door.

"Graham…" The pained expression on his face stopped her cold. "What's wrong? Is everything okay?"

"May I come in?"

"Of course. Sure." She stepped aside then closed the door behind him and followed him into the living room.

He didn't sit, instead he paced from the window to the couch and back again. His facial expression was tight and drawn.

"What's going on?"

"I got a call." He tugged his tie loose then slung his hands into his pockets. His jaw clenched and unclenched.

"O-kay." She looked at him in confusion. "From who?"

"A hospital in Barbados. It's my mother."

Her pulsed tripped. "What happened?"

"They asked that I come right away. She's in a coma. She has me listed as next of kin," he snorted a laugh. "Next of kin. Next to last of kin is more like it."

"Oh, Graham...I'm so sorry." She made a move to go to him, then stopped. He was one rigid surface. "You're going, right?"

He gritted his teeth, glared at her for a moment, then looked away. "No," he murmured.

Alexis studied him for a moment. She pushed out a breath and walked up to him. "If you've already made up your mind why did you tell me?" she gently asked.

Graham glanced up at her. "I came to you because I didn't know what else to do."

"What do you want to do?"

"I don't want to do anything because I don't want to be involved with her. I don't want to know anything that's wrong."

She pushed out a breath. "Then you *have* already made up your mind."

He lowered himself onto the love seat and rested his elbows on his thighs. "If it was up to you, what would you do?"

"If it was me I wouldn't be sitting here thinking about it. I would be on my way but that's where you and I are different. I can't tell you what you should do. You have to do what's in your heart."

"If I go according to what's in my heart I would go back up to my bedroom and go to sleep. The only way I can think about it is rationally because I don't know if I have any feelings for this woman who calls herself my mother. Why should I care about her now when she never cared about me for all of these years?"

"Only you can answer that, Graham."

"I don't know if I can, that's why I'm here. I need your help. I need you to help me think it through. You always have the ability to finish my thoughts or bring them into focus."

Alexis slowly sat down next to him. She took his hand and placed it in hers. "I can't tell you what to do, but if I were you I know that I would be going to see my mother. This may be the last time you get a chance to see her and there's nothing worse than living a life filled with regret, and you will regret it if you don't go. Yes, she's in a coma. But she could come out of it at any time and maybe that one time when she does wake up you would be there. Is that what you want to miss?"

He lowered his head. "I don't know what I want."

"This is a part of your life that you've been battling with for years. It's long past time that you came to some sort of resolution for yourself so that you can move on with your life."

"I'll go if you come with me."

She jumped up from her spot next to him. "Don't put this on me. I won't take that kind of responsibility. You have to go for yourself, not because I'm going."

"Let me put it another way," he said, "I *need* you to go with me." He squeezed her fingers in his hand. "Come with me. Please. I'm asking you."

She knew how difficult this was for him based on all of the things that he'd confessed to her about his relationship with his mother or lack thereof.

"It will give me a chance to show you my childhood home." He looked deep into her eyes, waiting.

Alexis folded her arms around her waist as if to protect herself from the sensual assault of his gaze. She turned away. She felt him behind her.

"You don't think I've noticed that things have been different between us?" he softly asked.

Her body tensed.

"Come with me, Alexis. I'll see my mother and hopefully you and I will have a chance to reconnect while we're away." He gently placed his hands on her shoulders and heat flowed through her. He turned her around to face him. He lifted her chin with the tip of his index finger and looked into her eyes.

And when she looked at him, when he touched her, said her name it was impossible for her to deny *him* or *her* need for him.

Chapter 19

The lilt of the Bajan flight attendants, the variety of island fare and fruity drinks made the four-and-a-half-hour flight from JFK International Airport to Grantley Adams International Airport in Barbados a pleasant diversion from the real reason for the trip.

For the first couple of hours of the flight, Graham made lighthearted conversation and commentary on the assortment of passengers, sharing jokes and island folklore against the backdrop of the newest James Bond flick. However, the closer they came to their destination, the less animated Graham became. His facial expressions grew tight, his body tense, his responses went from full sentences to one word answers to grunts of acknowledgement.

Alexis reclined her seat and closed her eyes. If this was the prelude to what the rest of the week would be like, then maybe she'd made a bigger mistake than she'd thought.

They deplaned and breezed through customs only to be stopped every ten feet by someone welcoming them to Barbados.

"Pretty friendly place," Alexis quipped as they walked behind the white-sleeved baggage attendant from the terminal out to the balmy air of the Caribbean. Graham didn't respond.

The initial view of Barbados was breathtaking to behold. It was a tropical paradise. Towering palms blew regally against the multicolored buildings, and the bright outfits of the natives and tourists gave the island an energetic vibe. The riot of colors and scents and musical cadence of the people was like stepping into the middle of a party that was in full swing.

"I want to go to the hotel first, freshen up, before..." His jaw clenched and his voice trailed off.

Alexis drew in a breath of resolve, determined to make the best of a difficult situation.

On the cab ride to the hotel the driver chatted nearly nonstop as he pointed out places of interest and places to avoid.

"So what brings ya to our beautiful 'rum' island? I sure hope it's pleasure, mon, 'cause we got plenty pleasure." He chuckled at his own joke.

Graham stared out of the window as the images flew by. Alexis watched when his nostrils flared, his brow creased or his lips flattened to a tight line. A montage of emotions played across his face. Maybe she was more wrong than she thought—and not about her accompanying him, but encouraging him to come at all. Clearly it was incredibly painful to come back here and the worst she was sure was yet to come.

Then suddenly he took her hand—the first time he'd touched her in hours—and gently squeezed it in his. His throat worked up and down as if the words were fighting to get out.

"Thank you," he said, his voice ragged. He brought her hand to his lips and tenderly kissed her knuckles without ever taking his eyes off the winding road.

Finally the cab came to a halt in front of The Grove Hotel and Resort in the parish of Christ Church. The sprawling complex was beachfront property with ocean views from nearly every vantage point.

Alexis gazed in appreciation of the scenic beauty that enveloped them. Everywhere that she turned each image was more brilliant and lush than the last.

The lobby of the hotel was an indoor Garden of Eden with white furnishings dotting the space. A fountain surrounded by brilliant-colored flora was the centerpiece of the lobby. The entire far wall was glass with a view of the brilliant blue water and white sand. It seemed that everyone was walking around with some kind of exotic drink in their hands. It was definitely the kind of atmosphere where one could put their troubles aside.

Graham took Alexis's hand while they walked to reception.

"Welcome to The Grove. You have a reservation?"

"Yes. Stone. Graham Stone."

The desk clerk put his name in the computer. "Yes, Mr. Stone. You reserved the suite for five days."

"Yes."

"How many keys would you like?"

"Two."

She typed in some information and his key cards were authorized. She handed him the cards. "You will be on the penthouse floor." She tapped the bell on the desk and a young man emerged from the back room. "Please help Mr. and Mrs. Stone to their room."

Alexis's breath caught for a moment at being referred to as Mrs. Stone. Graham grasped her hand a bit tighter and glanced briefly at her with a half smile on his lips. They followed the young man to the bank of elevators and rode to the penthouse floor.

The young man opened the double doors to their suite with a flourish and Alexis sucked in a breath at the view, which was magnificent—much like the lobby—with one wall a massive window that looked out onto the ocean and the horizon beyond. The space was completely an open floor plan with each space leading into the next separated only by the arrangement of furnishings, which again like the lobby was white with accents of turquoise and magenta.

"Your bedroom is in the back. There is a full bath and a guest bath, a full bar and living space with a dining area," the bellman detailed, showing them around. "Amenities are 24/7. There's a full-service gym, rooftop deck and indoor pool, and the restaurant is on the main level. Should you choose to dine, we do offer room service."

"Thank you, you've been very helpful," Graham checked the name tag, "Allen."

The young man gave a slight nod of his head. "I'm on duty until eleven should you need anything." He took a card from his shirt pocket and placed it on the counter.

"Thank you, Allen." Graham took out his wallet and handed him a twenty.

"Thank you, Mr. Stone." He tipped his head toward Alexis. "Mrs. Stone."

Once he was gone Graham said, "I hope you don't mind being call Mrs. Stone. It's simply easier not to have to explain."

What was she supposed to say that? "Whatever is easier," she replied drolly, turning away from him.

"Let's get unpacked and settled. Are you hungry?"

"Starving actually. Between the salt water and the delicious aromas..." She grinned and he smiled in return.

"Want to check the restaurant or would you prefer room service?"

"I am a bit tired. Room service is fine, but don't you want to go to the hospital first?" She could have sworn she saw a flash of fear dart across his face.

"I'll call now."

She headed off in the direction of the bedroom. The king-size bed dominated the space, but at least it would be roomy enough.

"I called the hospital. No change." Graham walked up behind her. "I guess I should not have assumed that we should share a room." He turned around. She kept her eyes lowered. "I was hoping that being together and away from everything we could get back to where we were." He stroked her cheek with the tip of his finger. "I miss you, Alexis. When I'm not with you..." He bent his head to kiss her behind her ear. Her breath hitched in her chest.

"I miss the feel of you in my bed every night, beneath me..."

Alexis's body warmed from the soles of her sandaled feet to the top of her head. Her heart beat faster. She knew she wanted him and that would never stop. She felt the same way he did. Without him at the end of the day she felt unanchored. But these mini-intermissions from real life, though thrilling beyond belief, were no longer enough. She wanted more and she knew that he wasn't signed up for that, but now wasn't the time to tell him that it all had to come to an end. She'd wait until they got through this visit, but when they returned to New York this madness had to end. Even as her body willingly opened for him, writhed beneath him exploded into tiny little pieces around him and her heart ached to belong to him, she promised herself that this crazy, undefined relationship would end. Somehow.

Chapter 20

After they'd showered and had a bite to eat, Graham called the hospital again. Alexis watched his expression shift as he listened.

"I understand. Yes. Thank you." He disconnected the call and looked off into the distance.

"What is it?"

"We should go," he said, quietly.

"Is she...?"

"No, but her doctor is coming on duty shortly and he wants to speak with me."

Guilt assailed her. She knew that had it been her own mother she would have made the plane land in the parking lot of the hospital. But Graham had a different relationship with his mother. He'd been reticent about this visit from the beginning. She could see him finding things to delay the inevitable the moment they'd landed—from going to the hotel instead of the hospital, ordering room service, making love. She should have pushed him to go the minute they set foot on the island. But she was in uncharted territory with Graham in this situation. She didn't want to push too hard and she didn't want to remain too distant either. She was there to support him and be his conscience when he needed it. Like now.

Alexis walked over to him and placed her hand gently on his arm. "We're doing this together," she said, softly. "You're not alone." Her gaze caressed his face.

He blinked bringing her into focus and the total look of adoration that was in his eyes filled her to overflowing. When he opened his mouth to speak she knew he was going to say the words that she'd longed to hear.

"I can't tell you how much your being here means to me." He kissed her softly on the lips.

She swallowed over the tight knot in her throat and offered a shadow of a smile. "We should go."

The cab ride was bumpy and long. The hospital, New Hope, was on the other side of the island. The farther away they drove from the hotel, the more the trees became the only attraction. The Crayola colors of the homes and manicured lawns dissolved into the rural outback of the island that was dominated by homes that weren't much more than shacks, and goats had the right of way on the road.

The cab finally pulled onto a narrow road and the hospital came into view. Graham paid the driver and they got out.

Graham stood still in front of the six-story building.

Finally he took one step and then another and pushed through the glass-and-wood door.

The interior was crowded with waiting patients that were seated along a wall with more in a smaller waiting room. It reminded Alexis of a neighborhood clinic rather than a hospital.

Graham strode over to the information desk. "I'm here to see...Paulette Braithwaite."

The clerk turned to her computer, typed in some information and then glanced up at him. "Sixth floor, ICU." She handed him a pass.

"Thank you." He hesitated for a moment as if contemplating his last chance to turn around.

Alexis slipped her hand in his. "Sixth floor," she gently coaxed. He nodded his head and they walked toward the elevator.

The ICU was one section of the sixth floor with no more than eight patients. The sound of beeping machines and the low hum of voices were the only sounds, a far cry from the main floor with its bevy of sights, sounds and odors.

Graham and Alexis walked over to the nurses' station. A beautiful young nurse with the most incredible coffee-bean complexion and eyes the color of rum greeted them.

"How may I help you?" Her voice was musical and took the sting away from where they were.

Graham cleared his throat. "Paulette Braithwaite."

The nurse checked her log book. "Yes, she's in room 6." She seemed to study Graham for a moment and then smiled. "You must be her son. You favor her."

Alexis felt Graham stiffen beside her. He didn't respond. Instead he turned toward room 6.

Paulette Braithwaite wasn't surrounded by flowers

and get-well cards. There wasn't a sign that anyone had
been there to see her besides hospital staff. Her company was the heart monitor and the oxygen mask that
helped to pump air into her lungs.

Graham stood in the frame of the doorway staring at
the imperceptible rise and fall of her chest beneath the
white sheet. The hiss and hum and rhythmic bleeping of
the machines added to the surreal quality of the moment.

Tenuously Graham approached his mother's bedside.
Alexis was near tears as she witnessed the array of emotions sweep across his face and grip his body; shock,
hurt, love, fear, loss and despair—they all volleyed for
a dominant position.

Graham tugged in two short breaths as if he was
suddenly having trouble breathing. He gripped the side
rails of the bed.

Paulette was a shadow of the woman he remembered
as his mum. It had been twenty years since he'd last seen
or spoken with her, but he remembered it as if it were
only yesterday.

He'd just turned seventeen and was finished with
school. He didn't know what he wanted to do with his
life beyond get away from the one he'd been living. He'd
grown accustomed to being alone, cast aside and overlooked. He no longer expected anything from anyone
and knew that he would have to find his own way. Growing up he'd retreated into a world of books to escape the
reality of his life that was filled with dreams of traveling
the world as far away from where he was as possible.

So when his birthday arrived he decided to join the
British Navy and see the world for free but was stopped
in his tracks for his underage status and the fact that he
was a U.S. citizen.

His aunt was useless in giving him any information, and even though she'd been the one to keep a roof over his head she'd never attained legal guardianship—his mother still had claim to him. He could simply wait another year until he turned eighteen and simply go on his own, but he didn't think he could survive another year.

Always industrious he'd been saving his money over the years and had stashed away a sizable sum of money for a seventeen-year-old—enough money for the ticket to Barbados and then the States with money to live on for a while. He was going to get his mother to sign the papers that would give him his freedom and cut all ties once and for all.

He wasn't sure what to expect when he walked up to the white and sky-blue house at the end of the road. He had a vague image of the house and it seemed smaller than he recalled.

There was a woman sitting on the porch smoking a cigarette. She reminded him of the actress Dorothy Dandridge but with a harder edge.

She shielded her eyes with her hand against the blaze of the sun as he approached.

"Whatevah ya sellin' I don't wan none."

Graham lifted his chin and walked forward. He stood on the bottom step.

"I done told ya, don't wan none of what ya sellin'."

"You don't know who I am, do you?"

She leaned forward a bit and a sudden flash of recognition lit her amber-colored eyes. Her lips trembled. And just as quickly the window of vulnerability shut.

"So what ya come 'ere for, money?"

"No."

She almost looked relieved. "So what then?" She lit

a fresh cigarette, inhaled deeply and blew a thick cloud of smoke into the air.

His insides knotted into a tight ball, the pain so intense he could hardly breathe. He wanted her to hug him, tell him that she loved him, tell him how sorry she was that she'd sent him away and that she was glad that he was home.

His eyes, so much like hers, burned with tears that he refused to shed. He dug into his backpack and pulled out the papers that required her signature and handed them to her.

"Just sign them and I'll be gone."

She took the paper, briefly scanned them through the smoke that wafted across her face and then looked at him with her hand out. "Pen."

Graham fished in his bag and gave her a pen.

Paulette signed the papers on three places giving "parental consent" for him to join the U.S. Navy. She handed them back to him. "Navy, huh?"

Graham nodded his head, his throat too tight to speak.

Paulette glanced away. She sniffed. "Take care of yourself."

Graham felt as if he'd been stabbed in the gut. "I always have." He turned away and never looked back.

"Graham." The sound of his name being called seeped beneath his consciousness and drew him back. He felt the weight of Alexis's hand on his arm. "The doctor is here," she was saying. He blinked her into focus and then noticed the doctor at the foot of the bed. He came around.

"I'm Dr. St. Clair," he said and extended his hand. Graham shook it mechanically, still shaken by the visceral memory. "You must be Mr. Stone."

"Yes, yes I am."

"We had a bit of a time trying to find you. She only listed your name as next of kin and that you lived in the States. When she was lucid she did mention that you were in the navy. They helped us to locate you."

"I'm not really sure what you want from me. I haven't seen her in twenty years."

"I understand. Can we talk outside?"

"I thought she was in a coma."

"No. She is heavily sedated. She's in a very, very deep sleep. They say that patients can still hear things around them even in that state." He smiled. "I believe that. And so I believe that what we say around them matters." He extended his hand toward the door.

Graham looked at Alexis and placed his hand on her waist. "Whatever you have to say you can say it in front of Alexis."

Alexis gave him a tight-lipped smile of encouragement.

"I'll be blunt," Dr. St. Clair said once they were in the hall outside of Paulette's room. "Your mother doesn't have long. It may be two weeks or it could be two months, but not much longer than that. The disease is too far gone. All we are doing now is making her comfortable."

Graham's jaw flexed. Alexis linked her fingers through his. "What's the plan?" He managed to ask.

"Keep her sedated. She's getting management through a feeding tube."

"Will she wake up?" His voice sounded hoarse.

"If we decreased the medication. Yes. Slowly. She can be roused. But the pain... I wouldn't recommend it, Mr. Stone."

Graham looked away. "Why did you want me here?"

"Mr. Stone, as your mother's doctor it was my moral and ethical responsibility to contact you. Yes, I could have told you all of this on the phone, but if we need to take any heroic efforts we want to make sure that the family is fully aware and has had an opportunity to see the family member for themselves especially if we have to make decisions." He paused for emphasis. "There are forms that need to be signed, as well."

"Let's get them signed," Graham said firmly.

More than an hour later, Graham and Alexis were in front of the hospital getting into a taxi to return to the hotel.

Graham was quiet and Alexis could see the thoughts and emotions race across his face, yet he didn't utter a word. He only held her hand and as much as she wanted to know what was on his mind and on his heart she understood that he needed time to process everything that was happening.

That night when they made love it was raw and fierce and wordless. It was Graham's body that spoke volumes. The pain in his heart poured into Alexis and she tried to absorb it, willing her own body to take some of his hurt away.

The next few days of their trip were filled with good times as well as difficult ones. They fell into an easy routine of breakfast on the terrace overlooking the ocean, shopping trips into town and doing all the touristy things, swimming in the ocean, fishing and riding Jet Skis. Alexis even did some underwater diving that was incredible, and they toured Crane Beach in the parish of St. Philip and hung out at St. Lawrence Gap—the strip for nighttime entertainment. They made exquisite, sweet, hard and passionate love whenever the mood hit them, and they visited his mother in the hospital.

In the four days that they'd been in Barbados Graham hadn't talked about his mother at all. When they went to see her, he'd ask the usual questions of the nurses regarding her state and then he would sit silently by her bedside for an hour and leave without ever saying a word or exhibiting an emotion.

Whenever Alexis tried to probe him he responded by saying that he didn't want to talk about it and he'd change the subject to some island folk story or sports or music or work. He even suggested bringing the R.E.A.L. concept to the island; anything but his mother.

They celebrated Thanksgiving on the beach under the fruit trees and stars with the waves lapping gently toward the shore and the sound of calypso music wafting through the air in the distance. They munched on breadfruit, and green bananas, stewed chicken, bakes and callaloo. It was a magical experience that Alexis would never forget. A perfect ending to a week of mixed emotions.

They had a two-o'clock flight back to New York on Friday afternoon. Their bags were packed including the extra luggage they'd had to buy to contain all of the souvenirs and extra clothing that they'd purchased. They would go straight to the airport from the hospital.

"All things considered, meaning the reason why we are here," Alexis began as she moved closer to Graham in the cab, "I enjoyed my visit. It's beautiful here." She took his hand and held it. "I'm hoping that at the very least you have added some pleasant memories to connect to your time here."

He turned to her and looked into her eyes. "Only

because of you," he said quietly. "Not really sure how I would have dealt with…all this if you had not been here. I know I've been—" he glanced away for a moment, searching for the word "—a real bastard about this whole thing with my mother." He chuckled mirthlessly. "Perfect word for what I've felt like most of my life."

"Graham…" she whispered, the ache evident in her own voice.

He shook his head. "No worries, I'm used to it really."

But she knew that he wasn't. Who could be? His entire life had been molded and framed by what his mother had done. Alexis felt that there was a part of him that believed he would never be good enough, so he strove for excellence in himself and everyone around him. He could have turned out completely different, a burden on society instead of an asset, but instead he used his adversity to propel himself forward rather than use it as a crutch. But without a doubt he may have found a way to excel out in the world but his heart was broken, his soul was an open wound and she wasn't sure what it would take for him to fully heal.

They arrived at the hospital and Graham had arranged with the driver to wait for them, assuring him that he would be fully compensated.

"Why don't you go on up and I'll get us some coffee," Alexis suggested.

He looked at her for an instant and she could have sworn that she saw a flash of panic in his eyes. In the days that they had been coming to the hospital they'd always sat in the room together; she off in the corner of the room and he sitting stoically next to his mother's bed for the designated hour. Alexis often wondered;

What are you thinking about? What do you see when you look at her?

"Uh, sure. I'll go on up," he said, each word stumbling out of his mouth.

Before she could respond he'd turned and walked toward the elevator.

Alexis walked in the opposite direction toward the concession stand and waited her turn. She took in the comings and goings, the sights and sounds inside the hospital and envisioned the island beauty beyond. What she realized was that she was filled with a mix of relief and regret that today was their last day. Relieved that she would not have to see Graham torture himself on a daily basis, but saddened that they should leave this beautiful place with so much still unresolved. The trip had taken its toll on her as well, although she hadn't mentioned anything to Graham, he had enough to deal with. But when she got back home she was definitely going to visit her doctor for some vitamins and a quick checkup. She'd always had trouble with anemia and with the crazy schedule that she'd been keeping over the past six months it was beginning to wear on her.

She got two coffees and went to meet Graham. The ICU was always more quiet than the rest of the hospital, with the staff and visitors understanding how important it was for tranquillity for the most ill patients.

When Alexis approached the open door of room 6 she stopped short when she heard Graham's voice and the pure pain in it tore right through her.

"Did you ever care what happened to me? Ever? Why didn't you come? Do you know I waited for you? I prayed that you would come for me, that you wouldn't leave me there with those people who never loved me, thought of

me as an inconvenience that they were saddled with."
His voice cracked. "But you never came. You never
wrote. Why did you give me up, Mum? Why? Do you
have any idea what that did to me?"

He pressed his head against the rails of the bed and
Alexis saw his shoulders and back tremble as his quiet
sobs rocked through him.

Her eyes clouded over and filled with tears that
streamed down her face. Quickly she turned away. She
didn't want him to see her and know that she had witnessed his most vulnerable moment. She went down the
hall to a corner to compose herself before returning to
the room and to give Graham the time that he needed.

When she returned he was standing and staring out
of the window. He didn't move until she was standing
right next to him.

"Hey, sorry I took so long." She handed him his coffee.

"Thanks. We'd better go," he said abruptly. His brows
knitted together as he looked at her. Then he kissed her
forehead and put his arm around her waist. "We have a
plane to catch."

They walked together past his mother's bed. He took
a brief look and she felt his body tense and then they
were gone.

Chapter 21

Graham and Alexis had the weekend to unwind and get their heads together for the return to work on Monday when Blake surprised them, saying that Sydni was in town and it would be great if they could get together for drinks or brunch on Sunday.

As much as Alexis wanted to simply crawl into bed, bury herself under her covers and sleep for a week she agreed to drinks Saturday night. She really wanted her Sunday to relax and recuperate. Alexis really liked Sydni and wished that she lived closer so that they could develop a real friendship. But as Sydni had said, if Alexis ever wanted to get away she was always welcome to visit her in Louisiana.

They'd settled on Rhythms, a jazz club in the city, for drinks. Blake recommended it, saying that his good buddy Nick Hunter owned it with his wife, Parris McKay, the jazz singer.

Alexis had to smile to herself. These two traveled in some well-heeled circles. She'd been listening to Parris's music for years.

Even as tired as she was she had to admit that she was happy she'd come along. Blake and Sydni were great to be around, just to see the happiness in their eyes when they looked at each other was contagious. And before long Graham's robust laugh, the sparkle in his eyes and the gentle way he touched her were back.

Maybe they could work it out, she thought wistfully as she watched his profile while he laughed at one of Blake's really corny jokes.

"You're in love with him, aren't you?" Sydni asked low enough for only Alexis to hear.

Alexis felt her face heat. She turned to Sydni with a shy smile on her face. "Is it that obvious?"

"To me it is." She laughed lightly. "But it's okay, your secret is safe with me. And safe from him, too, I take it."

Alexis exhaled slowly. "I'd like to keep it that way."

Sydni raised her glass in solidarity. "Us chicks have to stick together."

Alexis laughed and raised her glass. "Exactly."

After having been gone from the office for an entire week, even though the office had been closed, it was a bit hard to get up and running and back to speed. With Thanksgiving out of the way, the holiday season was in full swing and Christmas was on the horizon and the staff's focus was on planning holiday parties and winter getaways.

That was fine with Alexis. Things were slowing down

this time of year so she had an opportunity to get some appointments set up to visit a few of the schools before they closed for the holiday. She would get Claire to schedule those for her over the course of the next few weeks.

In the meantime, her doctor was able to squeeze her in for a late-afternoon appointment before *she* went on vacation.

"I'm heading out, Claire. I doubt I'll be back today. Anything urgent you know how to reach me."

"No worries. See you tomorrow."

Alexis hurried down the hall to catch the elevator but missed it and maybe for the best. She needed to use the restroom anyway.

As she was adjusting her clothes in the stall her name floated to her. She stiffened.

"She has no clue. He's using Alexis the same way he always does. Sleep with them and move on. She won't last much longer."

Alexis's heart pounded so loudly she could barely hear what they were saying.

"Really?"

"Yeah. Think about it. Think about the females that have worked here and are gone now. Coincidence?"

"True, but…"

"Trust me, *I* know."

"Really?"

"Yes, really."

"Nooo. You and Graham?" The voice rose in pitch. Tracy laughed. "Let's go."

Alexis heard the bathroom door close behind them. She was trembling so badly that she began to feel sick and threw up her lunch.

* * *

There was nowhere that she could go that Graham wasn't there—at work, at home. At least at work she could actively avoid him. At home it was more difficult and she didn't know how much longer she could keep it up without exploding.

She hadn't told anyone what she'd overheard in the ladies room, not even Naomi. She felt so used and dirty and she wasn't ready to share that humiliation with anyone, not even her best friend.

One evening about a week after the ladies room incident, she was at home and decided to take a look at her work contract. She knew it was for five years but if she was not mistaken there was also an opt-out clause, but she couldn't remember the exact details.

She looked through her files and located the contract. There it was, at the bottom of page five. *"Before the end of the six month probationary point either party shall have the option to continue or sever this agreement without penalty..."*

She sat back against the pillows on her bed. She had one more week to make the decision to stay or go. But the news she received the following morning made her decision that much easier.

Chapter 22

"Alexis, you have a call on line three," Claire said through the intercom.

"Thanks." She pressed down the flashing light on her phone.

"Alexis Montgomery."

"Hello, Ms. Montgomery. This is Dr. Sloan. I was wondering if you could come into my office this afternoon."

"This afternoon? Is something wrong?"

"No, but I want to discuss your test results with you."

"You're making me nervous."

"Don't be. Can you come in?"

"Sure. Um, I can be there in an hour."

"Perfect. See you then."

Alexis sat in the center of her bed. She'd cried enough to sink a ship. She'd wavered between disbelief, outrage and fear for hours. This was just not possible. It simply wasn't. But according to her doctor one in every 450 women found themselves in her position. The fact that she was anemic only helped to mask it.

What was she going to do? The bigger question was how did she even feel about being pregnant by a man— her boss—who didn't give a real damn about her, had abandonment issues and had no desire to settle down? She felt like crap. That's how she felt. Not to mention that she, the face of R.E.A.L. would be a lousy example to the kids and her clients and the staff.

"Oh, God!" she wailed and fresh tears flowed.

When Naomi called later that evening Alexis had pulled herself together enough to manage a conversation without breaking into a million pieces.

Naomi listened quietly until Alexis had exhausted herself. "What do you want to do, Lexi? Whatever you decide you know I have your back."

"I've been tormenting myself with that question since I walked out of my doctor's office. Of course I'm going to go through with it, but more than that…"

"Do you plan to tell Graham."

Alexis's heart felt like it seized in her chest. "No."

"Lexi, he deserves to know."

"Maybe. Not now. I just can't. And I don't want him making any demands or false promises or offering fake feelings. I don't want any of that crap!"

"Look, I know you're used to doing things on your own and being your own woman, but I'm telling you, sis, this is different. Way different."

"I'll handle it."

Naomi was quiet for a moment. "What do you need me to do?"

That gentle question brought fresh tears. "I sublet my place for six months." She laughed at the irony of it. "If you could make the calls, let them know I'll be back."

"Not a problem. When do you plan to come back to Atlanta?"

"I'm putting in my notice tomorrow. Two weeks. If the tenants need more time, I can stay in a hotel when I get back to Atlanta."

"All right. I'll take care of it and call you tomorrow."

"Thanks."

"And, Lexi…"

"Yes?"

"I love you, girl, and it's gonna be all right."

Alexis sniffed. "Love you, too."

Alexis took the elevator down to Graham's floor. Tracy nearly leaped out of her seat when she saw her coming.

"Ms. Montgomery, can I help you with something?"

"No. You've been helpful enough. Is he in?"

"Yes, I can buzz him."

"Don't bother." She breezed by her and walked into Graham's office without knocking.

He was just hanging up the phone when she walked in. He had a dazed look in his eye and it took him a moment to focus on her. He cleared his throat.

"Alexis, did we have an appointment?"

"No." Something was clearly wrong but she couldn't focus on whatever Graham's issues might be. She drew in a breath and walked up to his desk. "My six month probation is up and I'm submitting my letter of resignation." She handed it to him but he didn't move. He simply stared at her like she'd lost her mind. Finally he spoke.

"What?"

"My resignation. This is my two week notice. I'll be sure to tie up loose ends and get the apartment emptied."

His voice sounded as if it came from far away. "I should have followed my instincts and promoted from within." He glanced up at her with pure unadulterated fury and agony in his eyes. "There's no need for you to wait out the two weeks. Consider today your last day. That will give you plenty of time to clear out of the apartment." His nostrils flared as he sucked in air. He didn't look at her.

"I'll be gone by the end of the week."

"Fine." He dismissed her with a toss of his hand as if she was no more important than an annoying fly. He swung his chair around toward the window.

She spun away and walked out, holding back the tears that scorched her eyes.

When Alexis returned to her office, she'd shaken off the shock of the hurt of his callous dismissal, which was replaced by resolve. She summoned Claire into her office and broke the news to her, answered the minimal amount of questions, assured her that she would be reachable by phone if there were any questions and that she was sure that the transition would be a smooth one.

"I...understand," Claire said on a breath, clearly shaken by the news. "I'd really hoped that you would stay on. Everyone loves you here."

Alexis's throat clenched. *Everyone except Graham and Tracy.* "Thank you for that." She forced a tight smile. "I'm going to clean up my desk, close out some files," she said by way of letting Claire know that she needed some time. "I'll be sure to see you before I leave."

Claire nodded, tight-lipped and walked toward the door.

"Claire…"

She turned around. "Yes?"

"I don't want anyone to know. I'm sure Mr. Stone will discuss it at the staff meeting."

She nodded solemnly and closed the door softly behind her.

Alexis felt like she was going to shatter. But she didn't. She forced herself to focus on the tasks at hand. Within the hour, she had responded to email, saved files and shut down her computer. She stopped at Claire's desk on her way out.

"Thank you for everything," she said, quietly.

"I wish things could be different," Claire said.

Alexis forced a smile. "Take care of yourself and I'm only a phone call away."

She walked out into the frigid December air and contemplated what her new life was going to look like.

Chapter 23

Fortunately Alexis only spent a week in a hotel and by the third week in December she was back in her old place. All around her everyone was preparing for Christmas, but the Christmas spirit was the last thing she had on her mind.

Naomi had invited her to come and stay with her for a while but she'd declined. She still wasn't ready to mix and mingle and she certainly didn't want to be a third wheel in her friend's marriage.

Funny, she'd never been heartbroken before, she thought idly. Certainly she'd broken some hearts along the way but she had no idea that anything could hurt this bad. What could she have done differently?

Many a night she stared up at the ceiling with her hand pressed to her stomach wondering if she did the right thing by not telling Graham about the baby, or not confronting Tracy for the trash-talker that she was. But she wouldn't reduce herself to that. Somehow she'd work it out. She knew she would.

It was ten days until Christmas and she was going through her bookshelf deciding on which books she would donate to the local library when her cell phone rang.

She plucked it from her pant pocket. Her eyes widened in surprise.

"Sydni. Hi."

"Hi, yourself. How are you?"

Alexis wasn't sure how much she should say based on what Sydni knew or didn't know with Graham and Blake being best friends.

"I'm good."

"I heard you were back in Atlanta."

"Yes. For a few weeks now." *She had to have heard it from Blake who heard it from Graham. What else did he reveal?*

"New York isn't for everyone. I know it's a great place to visit, but I couldn't live there." She laughed lightly. "Listen, I know this is really last minute but my family is hosting their annual holiday party at my uncle Branford's home in Baton Rouge. I've missed the past couple of years but I'm determined to go this year and I'd love for you to join us."

"Oh, Sydni, that's really nice of you but I couldn't."

"Couldn't or wouldn't?" she said in a teasing voice.

"I'm really going to stay close to home for the holidays, but thank you so very much for thinking of me."

"Well, if you change your mind, you know how to

reach me. By the way, let me get your info, so that I can update my contact list."

Alexis gave her mailing info and the number to her landline.

"So are you back to work at the University?"

"No. Just weighing my options at the moment."

"Oh, okay. Well, listen, if you ever think of changing careers and working on branding and development, give me a call. I'm always looking for good people."

Alexis laughed. "I'll keep that in mind."

"I guess you heard that Graham's mother passed."

Her breath caught. "No... I hadn't. When?"

"December 6."

She blinked. Her brows drew together. *The sixth.* That was the same day she handed in her resignation. He'd looked upset when she came in. He'd just gotten off of a call. *Could that have been...*

"Well, you have a great holiday and remember it's never too late to change your mind."

"You, too, and I'll try to remember that."

"You have my card so anytime..."

"Thanks. Take care, Sydni."

"You, too."

Alexis disconnected the call. She really did like Sydni. If things were different she wouldn't have hesitated to take a trip to Louisiana. But things *were* different. And she was pretty sure that Graham would be invited, as well. She wasn't ready to see him and she didn't know when she would be.

Alexis wondered how he was taking the news about his mother? Had he gone back to Barbados? Did he finally find peace? The questions tumbled all over each other in her head with no end in sight. The only thing she could do was put it all out of her mind as much as possible. She had enough to worry about.

Naomi called just about every day trying to convince her to join them for Christmas, and Ian had gotten wind that she was back in town and wanted to get together. She put that off, too.

It was about a week before Christmas and she was getting anxious about an order for a new mattress and box spring that she'd ordered for her bedroom to replace the one that had been used while she'd sublet her town house. Sleeping in the guest room was getting old.

She was just getting out of the shower when the door-bell rang. "Finally," she muttered. She grabbed an over-size T-shirt from the hook and put on her robe before going to the front door.

She looked through the panes of glass at the top of the door and her heart stood still, then began to beat so fast she couldn't breathe. She turned away from the door and squeezed her eyes shut.

The bell rang again and the shock of it ran through her like a bolt of lightning. She pressed her hand to her chest to still her racing heart, took a deep breath, turned around and opened the door.

When she stood in front of him, looked up into his eyes and saw the expression of joy on his face, all the weeks, all the uncertainty, the loneliness, the indecision—none of it mattered. Nothing mattered beyond the fact that Graham was standing there in front of her and not because he knew about the baby. There was no way for him to know and realizing that lifted her heart.

"Hi," he said so softly it was like a caress.

"Hi." Her voice broke.

"Please don't cry." He crossed the threshold and

pulled her tightly into his arms. "Don't cry, luv." He
buried his face in her hair. "I've done enough to make
you cry but I swear I'll never make you cry again."

She held on to him like a drowning woman holding
on to a life raft. She pressed her head against his chest
and the beat of his heart was the music of her life that
had been missing.

Finally, reluctantly they eased apart enough to come
fully inside.

"I can't believe you're here. What are you doing
here?" she asked in utter awe.

He shrugged out of his coat and hung it on the coatrack
near the door.

She took his hand and led him into the living room.

Graham looked around in admiration. "This space
is totally you." He sat down next to her on the couch.

She curled her legs beneath her and faced him, her
face aglow with happiness. "So…tell me."

His face sobered. "Maybe I should show you first and
then…" He reached into his jeans pocket and took out a
small envelope and handed it to her.

She stared at it in confusion. The envelope was ad-
dressed to him.

"Go ahead. Read it."

The envelope had already been opened. She took the
pages out and smoothed out the folds. She glanced at
him then began to read…

My son,
If you are reading this then I am gone and it's
good. No more suffering and living with the guilt
of what I have done.
    It wasn't because I didn't love you. It was be-

cause I did. I know that may be hard to understand. I lived a bad life, son. A bad life and I didn't
want it spilling on you. I knew your aunt would
give you a life as best as she could and whatever
struggle you had would make you strong. I know
she wasn't no loving woman. Didn't have a loving
bone in her body, but I believed that even that was
better than living with me.

I only hope you can forgive me someday. I
know all about the great life you made for yourself and all of those children. You turned out to
be a good man in spite of everything. Don't ever
forget that. I hope that one day you will find someone that is worthy of you and that one day you will
have a family of your own to love with all that I
know you got in your heart.
I'll always be watching.
Your mother

By the time Alexis came to the end of the letter the
words had become blurred and clouded. She wiped at
her eyes and sniffed hard and with reverence she re-
folded the letter.

She blinked away the rest of her tears and handed
him the letter. "How do you feel about what she said?"

He gazed up at the ceiling for a moment then focused on the letter in his hands. "Free. Like an enormous weight has been lifted from my soul."

A slow smile moved across her mouth. She reached
out and tenderly cupped his cheek in her palm. He took
her hand and held it against his face.

"Being abandoned left a hole in me that never seemed
to be filled. It was like a hunger." He chuckled soberly.

"I tried it with food. Excelling in everything. Taking on the futures of thousands of kids. None of it worked until I found you. But I still believed that I wasn't worthy and I wouldn't risk opening myself up for that kind of hurt. So I kept up a wall, Alexis, and you kept finding a way to scale it, pull the bricks down and get on the other side."

Alexis was shaking inside. This was what she wanted, wasn't it? This was what she'd dreamed of, wasn't it?

"The day you turned in your resignation was the same day I got the news about my mother." He shook his head as the memories washed over him. "I didn't think that I would care or that it would hurt the way that it did. And then you came in and all I could think of was that women that you love will hurt you and they will leave."

Alexis's pulse jumped in her veins.

"But you didn't leave me. You were there every step of the way. I pushed you away by not giving you what you deserved—to be loved and honored and adored. Totally and completely." Graham gathered Alexis to him. "I love you, Alexis. From the depths of my soul I love you. I'm only filled up when you are in my life." He tilted his head back and looked into her eyes. "I love you."

Alexis finally released the breath that she'd held. "I love you. I've loved you from the moment I set foot in the car. Well, maybe lust," she said, giggling with joy. "I love you, Graham Stone."

"I needed to hear you say that." He swallowed. "And I needed to be in a place where I could say this." He reached in his jacket pocket and took out a stunning diamond ring in a platinum setting. "Say yes. Say you will marry me. Be my friend, my partner, fill my soul."

Alexis could barely get her throat to work. "Yes. Yes. Yes."

Epilogue

Alexis held her left hand out in front of her and admired the dazzling diamond as it picked up the light from the moon. She turned onto her side and draped her bare leg across Graham's thigh.

"How are we going to work the logistics of this relationship?" Alexis asked. She ran a finger across his chest.

Graham tucked his hand beneath his head. "Two choices really. You can come back to New York as my wife and take your old job back and help me build my educational empire. Or I can make you my wife right here and I can relocate."

"How can you relocate? You have a business to run."

"Claire is more than capable. I can promote her to Assistant VP She's been with me from the beginning and can handle the day-to-day operations. She knows the business inside out. She deserves it."

"I totally agree. But what about Tracy? I'm sure she feels she deserves it, especially now that I'm gone."

"Tracy is no longer with the company. It seems that she had a real talent for spreading malicious rumors and slandering someone very important to me. In addition to which she's been pushing the line of propriety for a while, even going so far as to turn up at my apartment unannounced. She finally talked to the wrong person."

"Claire."

"Yes."

Inwardly Alexis smiled.

"Claire came to me and then several others at Claire's insistence. Essentially, Tracy's viciousness and rumor-spreading was causing a hostile work environment. Rather than fight the charges, she resigned." He shrugged. "End of story."

"Claire deserves that spot, whether you decide to move here or whether I move to New York." She paused, thought about how she should tell him. "Besides, I'll have to stop working anyway. I'll have plenty to keep me busy in about seven months."

Graham sat up. His hot gaze ran over her face and down to her belly then back up to her face to see her grinning in delight.

"You… We're… Are you saying… Serious?"

She nodded vigorously.

Graham's face broke into a grin so bright that it lit the room. And then he was above her gazing down into her face.

"I want you to come home with me for Christmas," he said with sudden urgency.

"New York. Fine. Of course."

"No. Home. Barbados. I want our baby to know its

roots from the very beginning. Christmas is a time of hope and renewal. Since we are going to be starting a new life I want to start at the beginning and paint a new future for the three of us."

He caressed her cheek with awe. He kissed her lips with a new tenderness, stroked her hip in homage and whispered her name in adoration.

"But first...I am going to make love to my soon-to-be wife and mother of my soon-to-be child. What do you say to that, soon-to-be Mrs. Stone?"

Alexis linked her fingers behind his head. "I can't wait."

* * * * *

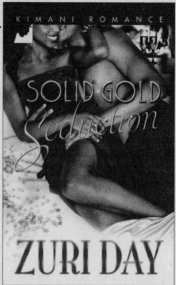

REQUEST YOUR FREE BOOKS!

2 FREE NOVELS
PLUS 2 FREE GIFTS!

KIMANI™
ROMANCE

Love's ultimate destination!

KROM13R

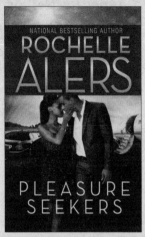